und Andere, Anne Eliot

Stories of New York

und Andere, Anne Eliot

Stories of New York

ISBN/EAN: 9783744750097

Printed in Europe, USA, Canada, Australia, Japan

Cover: Foto ©Andreas Hilbeck / pixelio.de

More available books at **www.hansebooks.com**

STORIES FROM SCRIBNER

STORIES OF
NEW YORK

NEW YORK

CHARLES SCRIBNER'S SONS

1893

STORIES OF NEW YORK

FROM FOUR TO SIX

A COMEDIETTA   BY ANNIE ELIOT

—

THE COMMONEST POSSIBLE STORY

BY BLISS PERRY

—

THE END OF THE BEGINNING

BY GEORGE A. HIBBARD

—

A PURITAN INGÉNUE

BY JOHN S. WOOD

—

MRS. MANSTEY'S VIEW

BY EDITH WHARTON

FROM FOUR TO SIX

By Annie Eliot

A COMEDIETTA IN ONE ACT

ESTHER VAN DYKE. HAROLD WHITNEY.
A MAID.

ESTHER *discovered seated in a New York drawing-room. She has been reading and tearing old letters.*

E. I am sure one might ask anyone to an afternoon tea, even if anyone were one's old lover ; and I am sure one might come to anyone's afternoon tea, even if anyone were one's quondam sweetheart. From both Harold's stand-point and mine, it seems to me perfectly safe. Certainly the vainest man could not believe that a woman wished to rake up the leaves of a dead past because she sent him an At-home from four to six card, for a day when she is to be at home for two hundred people besides. If it were an evening party, now—in summer with the lawn, or in winter with a conservatory— or if there is not a conservatory there are always stairs ; and it's daily more and more the fashion to build them curved. Another generation may find discreet recesses at every landing. When people are really thoughtful there will be a temporary addition where people can go up and down. Oh, if it was an evening party I could not blame Harold for staying away. Or if it was private theatricals —the stage is itself one grand opportu-

nity! Or a picnic—what innumerable
openings for raking up the dry leaves of a
dead past on a picnic! But an afternoon
tea! Nothing stronger or dryer than tea-
leaves to be had. Harold need not be in
the least afraid. Besides, it would have
been really unfriendly not to send him a
card. Everybody knows he is at home
again, and from a four years' trip. Even
after all that has passed I would not wish
to be unfriendly. Four years, and they
say that he is engaged to Mattie Montgomery — and just before he went away
he was engaged to me. (*A little sadly.*)
Perhaps he was foolish. Perhaps—I was.
Undoubtedly we both were. I suppose I
ought to feel flattered that he waited four
years—but somehow I don't—altogether;
" flattered " does not seem to be the word.
Well, it makes little difference now, and
it will make less when I tell him to-morrow that I am engaged to Dr. Tennant.
I thought I might as well look over his

letters. I have burned all but the last.
(*Takes up letter from the table.*) Here it
is. (*Takes up a second letter.*) And here
is Dr. Tennant's first. Two models of
epistolary communication—but of different orders. (*Reads.*)

"MY DEAR MISS VAN DYKE : I shall
give myself the pleasure of calling upon
you this afternoon at five o'clock. It rests
with you whether or not this pleasure is
to be intensified a hundredfold, or at-
tended with lasting pain. I remain always,
"Yours most cordially,
"EDWARD TENNANT."

What could be better suited to the circumstances than that ? Not too impas-
sioned, but sufficiently interested. I am
always affected by well-turned phrases—
I think this is charming. And here is
Harold's. (*Reads other letter.*)

"You have made it plain enough.
There is no necessity for more words.
Heaven forgive you—and good-by."

(*Thoughtfully.*)   He was in a pretty passion when he wrote that—and I have not
seen him since.   I hope he will come to-
morrow.   He used to think Mattie Montgomery was a doll of a thing.   Perhaps he
will tell her that I am a—no, he won't.
Whatever I am, I'm not a doll of a thing,
and he knows it.   (*Looks at the two letters
side by side.*)   How amusing one's old
flirtations look in the light of a new and
serious reality—for I have made up my
mind what to say to Dr. Tennant.   It will
be rather good fun to tell Harold of it
confidentially to-morrow.   I will drop it in
his tea with a lump of sugar.   (*Glances at
clock.*)   After four o'clock.   Well, I must
go and make myself fascinating and give
orders that Dr. Tennant and I are not to
be disturbed.   We may as well begin to
get used to *tête-à-têtes*.   (*Exit after putting the letters under a book, out of sight.*)

Enter HAROLD WHITNEY. *He seems disturbed.*

H. This is certainly confoundedly odd. I expected to find fifty other people here at least, and Esther in her best gown receiving them. I can't have mistaken the hour. It is some time after four. There is certainly a mistake somewhere, however, and under the circumstances it is likely to be a particularly awkward one. I would walk a good mile and a half to avoid a *tête-à-tête* with Esther Van Dyke. Because I have been fool enough after four years to remember the color of her eyes, I don't care to have her know it and see it. I would leave now, like the historic Arab, if I hadn't been such an ass as to give my card to the servant, and Esther has seen it by this time. I would rather face the music than give her the pleasure of laughing at me for running away. But what does it mean? I must—the blood curdles in my veins at the thought—I must have mistaken the day! The Fate which I have felt dogging my footsteps from the cradle has at last laid hold upon me! I have dreamed of getting to a place the day before I was asked. I have loitered irresolutely on door-mats. I have gone slowly by and watched until I saw another carriage go in, but I have never *done* it before. And to have come to Esther Van Dyke's after four years, and such a parting, a day too soon! My bitterest foe would find it in his heart to pity me now What can I do? (*Walks around the room and fingers things restlessly.*) I might go off with the spoons to divert suspicion. I would rather be arrested as a professional burglar, entering the house under false pretences, than witness Esther's smile when she comes to a realizing sense of what I have done. Professional burglars probably retain their self respect. There is no reason why they shouldn't. The

date of *their* visit is not fixed by invitation. But, confound it! there won't be
any spoons until to-morrow. Perhaps she
won't know I have come a day too soon—
but she always did know things—that was
the kind of person she was. (*Takes up a
book from the table.*) I might read to com-
pose my mind. "Familiar Quotations,"
—I wish I could find an elegant and ap-
propriate one for the occasion. I can
think of several, entirely familiar to the
most unlearned, but too forcible for a
lady's drawing-room. "Too late I stayed"
would hardly do. I wonder what the
fellow would have sung if "Too soon
he'd come." (*Throws down book.*) I
thought I could accept an invitation to an
afternoon tea, because I need only say a
word to her, see if she had changed, and
leave. That seemed safe enough. Besides, Miss Montgomery chaffed me about
coming, and wouldn't have hesitated to
make the most of it if I had stayed away.

....

(*Looks about.*)   The room has not changed much.   I wonder—here she is.   Now, for all I have learned in four years, I would like to conceal myself in the scrap-basket, but it is out of the question.

Enter ESTHER.

E. How do you do, Mr. Whitney? I am very glad to see you.   (*They shake hands.*)

H. It is very good of you to say so, Esth—Miss Van Dyke. (*Aside.*) I never felt so fresh in my life.

E. It was nice of you to think of coming this afternoon instead of waiting until the crush to-morrow, when I should have an opportunity for no more than a word with you.

H. (*aside*). She does not *look* satirical. Why didn't I bring some flowers or something? (*They sit.   Aloud, with somewhat exaggerated ease of manner.*) When one's hostess receives all the world, one's own reception cannot be a personal one. After four years I wished for something more positive. Perhaps I have been too bold, but an afternoon tea is so very impersonal, you know.

E. (*a little embarrassed by his manner, aside*). Can it be that he does not wish our relations to be impersonal ? Of course not ! (*Aloud.*) Yes, I know. Very impersonal indeed. I was thinking the same thing before you came.

H. (*aside*). Yes, and I was thinking the same thing before I came. We haven't either of us gotten on much. (*Aloud.*) I was always an exacting sort of fellow, you know, so you will not be surprised at my coming to get a reception on my own account.

E. (*aside*). I should think I did know. (*Aloud.*) No, I am not surprised. (*A moment's pause—with a slight effort.*) So you are an exacting sort of fellow still ? I am looking for the changes of four years, you see.

H. (*significantly*). You may not find many, after all. (*Somewhat gloomily.*) The rose - color wears off one's glasses somewhat in four years, to be sure, but I don't think the perspective changes much.

E. Don't you? It strikes me that time reverses the glasses — that we find ourselves suddenly looking through the other end, and things that once were so large are a long way off, and have become extremely small.

H. (*aside*). Which means, I suppose, that I have taken a back seat, and must keep at opera - glass distance. (*Aloud.*) Things have no importance of their own, then? I suppose it is a good deal a matter of which way you look at it.

E. Yes, education does everything for us — which is something of a platitude. But I am sorry about the rose-color. I'd much rather you should look at me through tinted glasses. I said the other day to a confidential friend that my complexion is no longer what it was.

H. (refusing to be diverted). No, I do not think one's views of persons change —or perhaps I should say one's attitude toward persons—as do those of abstractions. One does not expect to find truth — trust — honor — *love*, growing so large.

E. (soberly). In other words, truth is a hot-house, and one's ideas are tropical. Well, it is perhaps as well to come out into the open air, even if things do seem a little—stunted—at first.

H. Undoubtedly. Yet the comfort of the human frame demands something in the way of a temperate zone between. A sudden plunge into the arctic regions is apt to convey a chill—quite a serious one sometimes.

E. (aside). I wonder if that is meant for a veiled allusion. (*Aloud.*) But nature generally provides a way of softening matters, and makes such changes not chilling, but bracing.

H. (*carelessly*).   Yes—Nature has been much maligned in her time, but, after all she is kinder than humanity in certain of even its most attractive forms.   She is impartial and she contrives to let one down easily.   I am sometimes astonished that Nature should be personified as a woman.

E. (*looking away from him*).   I see you have become a cynic.

H. (*with intention*).   I have, perhaps, lived up to my opportunities.   They have not been unfavorable to cynicism.   (*Laughing.*)   Do you know, Esther, this is very much the way we used to talk ?   We were continually dealing in the most artistic abstractions.   How easily one drops into old fashions !

E. (*aside*).   How can he speak so lightly of " the way we used to talk," or is it only I that remember ?   (*Aloud, coldly.*) Possibly, but old fashions are very readily

seen not to belong to the present day.
And yet—I may be mistaken—but it seems
to me that we used to talk in a way that
bordered on—on the concrete.

H. (a little nonplussed). Yes—that is
true—but we were not so successful there.
(*Aside.*) Decidedly we did. On the very
concrete, indeed! And that was where
she always had the better of me. She is
quite capable of doing it again—but she
does not wish to.

E. (calmly). But where were we in
our abstractions? Ah, with Nature. I
always get beyond my depth when Nature is introduced into the conversation.
Human nature I do not mind at all, you
know, but Nature by itself frightens me.
I think it is the capital N. I feel that I
ought to go out-of-doors and appreciate
her.

H. I remember you were always afraid
of getting beyond your depth. I was less
prudent, however, which was sometimes

unfortunate. (*Aside.*) I shall be floundering again if I go on with this remembering. (*Aloud.*) So you are still cautious? I have not had the four years to myself. Have they not changed *you* at all, Esth— Miss Van Dyke?

E. (*pensively*). Yes.

H. (*with attention*). You are not quite the same, then? I should not have known it.

E. (*with emphasis*). Wouldn't you, really?

H. Unfortunately for me—no.

E. No, I am not the same.

H. (*in a low tone*). Will you tell me how you have changed?

E. (*after a pause*). I have grown stout! Yes, I have. I have gained twenty pounds in the four years you have been away.

H. (*laughing*). The inference pains me deeply. But twenty pounds can be judiciously distributed without actual in-

jury to the possessor.   Is there anything
else ?

E. (sentimentally).   Ah, yes, when I am
introduced to a new man I no longer expect to find him a mine of entertainment.
I used to.   Now I am surprised if I have
not to be clever for both of us.

H. Is that so new ?   (*Thoughtfully.*)   I
sometimes think I was stupid for both of
us—or—could it have been only that you
were too wise ?   (*Aside.*)   Oh, this fatal
tendency to reminiscence—and I know
better !

E. (with a slight effort).   You are carrying me too far back.   I am marking my
progress since I saw you.   (*Aside.*)   Certainly this is too much like burrowing in
the leaves of a dead past.   No wonder he
did not wait until to-morrow.

H. Forgive me, and go on with the dis-
illusionments.

E. Sadder yet, I no longer care when a
younger and a fairer girl " cuts me out,"

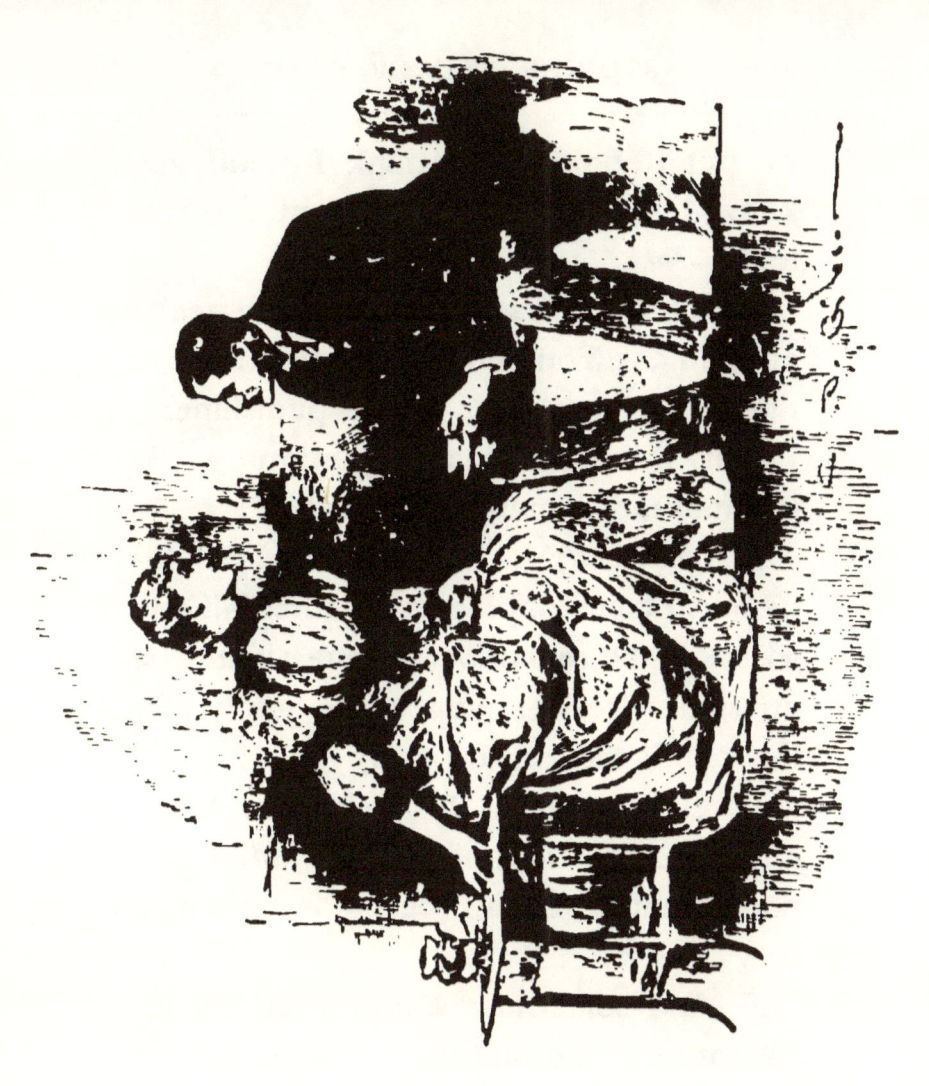

to put it boldly.   I think I shall, you know, but I don't.   I sigh—but I forget them—*both!*

H. This shows a callousness really alarming.   You might at least reserve the guiltier party for future punishment. Perfidy merits at least remembrance.   It is sometimes a man's last hold.

E. (carelessly).   A man should risk little on so commonplace a resource—if one wishes to be remembered, one should be unusual.   Besides, you would imply that the man is the guiltier party?

H. Only as far as his lights are taken into consideration, of course.   Man is a poor creature at his best — in comparison.

E. And sometimes a comparatively innocent one.   To find another woman more attractive is blamable, but to be a more attractive woman ought to be unpardonable.

H. " To err is human—fiendish to outshine." I understand. (*With marked politeness.*) Permit me to suggest that it is rarely——

E. (*laughing*). But I have said I have lost my capacity for feeling thrusts of this kind. (*In a lower tone.*) At least, I believed that I had.

H. (*dryly*). I was always a little unfortunate in my attempts to make amends —always too late, perhaps.

F. (*meeting his eyes*). Yes, making amends was never your forte.

H. Any more than cherishing illusions is yours. But, pray, go on with your revelations. I must improve the unexpected pleasure of finding you alone.

E. (*a little embarrassed*). Whom, then, did you expect to find here? (*Aside.*) He cannot have known that Dr. Tennant is coming. (*Aloud.*) Who would interfere, did you think, with the personal welcome you so desired?

H. (*aside*). I was getting on so well.

(*Lightly.*) Oh, party calls, you know, and——

E. (*dryly*). You will find that *customs* have not changed so much in four years. It is still unusual to pay party calls in advance.

H. (*aside*). That was a brilliant way to recoup my falling fortunes ! (*Boldly.*) Is this an indirect way of blaming me for coming this afternoon ? (*Rising.*) I suppose it was unwise. (*Aside.*) I should rather think it was. (*Aloud.*) I will go now—Esther.

E. (*quickly*). You know, Harold, I did not mean anything so rude. Do not go —unless you must.

H. (*aside*). I must—theoretically. But I sha'nt—not after that " Harold." If I hadn't prided myself for years on its being inalienable property, I should say I was losing my head. (*Aloud.*) Will you tell me more of your four years ?

E. (*seriously*). Yes. I have grown wise. I have grown hard—a little.

H. (*softly*). You were hard before—a little.

E. Are they not the same—wisdom and hardness ? I have learned to believe that they are.

H. (*impulsively*). Not always.

E. And I, too, have acquired the sense of proportion. I have seen that—that— Love is not all the world. I have learned that the comfortable is more to be desired than gold—yea, than fine gold.

H. Yes ; Gold and Love must both be tried in the furnace, which is seldom a comfortable operation.

E. And you—do you not agree with me ? Is it not better to look on ?

H. So long as it is not at another's happiness that one has desired for one's self—yes.

E. (*aside*). How if it be another's unhappiness, I wonder. Poor Dr. Tennant. (*Sighs.*)

H. (*aside*). I shall make an ass of myself in a moment. She is not changed an atom. (*Aloud.*) But what leaves of wisdom have you steeped for me? I expected a cup of tea, and you have given me a decoction that should heal all disappointments.

E. (*half sadly*). If I had known I possessed such a secret I should have brewed some for myself before this. But (*rising*) if you expected a cup of tea you shall have it.

H. (*eagerly*). By Jove! Esther! I beg pardon—but Miss Van Dyke, I beg of you—— (*Stops helplessly.*)

E. I was just about to send for it for myself. (*She rings. Aside.*) I see it all. He has come a day too soon. And he would have had me believe that he cared to see me alone. And I was actually growing sentimental. He shall pay for it. (*Enter a maid.*) Tea, Mary Ann.

H. (*who has been fidgeting about the room—aside*). If only I had gone half an hour ago—in the flush of triumph, as it were! It was unnecessary, in order to avoid making a sentimental spectacle of myself, to fall back upon the larder!

E. (*going back to table and taking up a letter*). Do you know what I was doing when you came this afternoon?

H. Learning a new Kensington stitch? Studying a receipt-book? Putting a man out of his misery by letter? These are, I believe, some departments of " woman's work."

E. No, I was reading an old letter— one by which a man put himself out of misery. Your last letter, in fact.

H. My last letter?

E. Yes.

MARY ANN *brings in the tea, and as* ESTHER *moves things on the table, she hands him* DR. TENNANT'S *letter by mistake.* HAR-OLD *glances at it and looks up surprised, but* ESTHER *does not see him.*

H. Am I to read this?

E. Certainly.

MARY ANN *leaves the room.* ESTHER *busies herself with the tea-things.*

H. (having read the letter — stiffly). Very elegant penmanship.

E. (surprised but indifferently). I had not thought of that. (*A pause.*)

H. (glancing at the letter again). I fancy the writer did.

E. (coldly). Possibly. (*Aside.*) Oh, why did I show it to him? I would not have believed he would be so hard. (*Aloud.*) Rather a forcible style, I think.

H. Stiff, rather than forcible, I would suggest.

E. (with suppressed feeling). Your criticisms are less pointed than usual. If you had said unnatural it might express your meaning still better.

H. (a little irritated). He is a fortunate man who is able to express himself with such justness and freedom from exaggeration.

E. It seemed to me exaggerated at the time.

H. (*with mock admiration*). Oh, how can you say so! It is positively Grandisonian—almost Chesterfieldian. (*Aside.*) And utterly detestable.

E. (*almost with tears*). I was wrong to fancy you would be interested in such a trifle. Please give it back.

H. (*politely, handing it to her*). Not at all. Certainly, the writer deserves the lasting happiness he refers to. (*Aside.*) And I wish it were nothing to me—if he gets it or not.

E. What do you mean? Is this what I gave you? Oh, dear! (*Much embarrassed.*) It was the wrong one! Never mind. Here is your tea.

H. (*takes the cup, after a short pause*). I feel as if I had forced myself into your confidence.

E. You need not. It was my own stupidity, of course.

H. (*tastes* ● *tea*). Might I see the other one ?

E. Yes. (*Gives it to him.*)

H. (*reads it while* ESTHER *watches him*). Yes ; well, I might have said more. But that was enough.

E. Yes, that was, as the children say, a great plenty. Oh, I neglected your tea ! One lump, or two ?

H. (*thoughtfully*). One. I wonder .if it has ?

E. What has ?

H. Heaven.

E. Heaven has what ?

H. Forgiven you.

E. I think so, by this time. It doesn't bear malice. Cream ?

H. Yes—prussic acid—anything. Thank you. You do not ask whether I have or not.

E. No. I understood you shifted the responsibility once for all. (*Sipping her tea.*)

H. Perhaps I did. It⬤ generally once
for all with me.

E. Is it ? It is better to have all—for
once. It is broader. It is more liberal.
It is my motto.

H. Yes. So it was then. I have heard
there is safety in numbers. (*Aside.*) If I
believed that, I should begin to repeat the
multiplication-table. I shall never be in
greater need of it.

E. Not always.

H. (*with an effort*). Possibly Sir
Charles Grand — I mean Mr. Edward
Tennant—may have a narrowing influ-
ence. (*Aside.*) It is no use. I can't be
discreet. Confound Mr. Edward Tennant !

E. (*innocently*). Perhaps. (*Drinks tea.*)
And so you are engaged to Mattie Montgomery ?

H. (*formally*). You do me too much
honor.

E. Really ! (*More coolly.*) That is a

pity. I hoped we might proffer mutual congratulations. An exchange of compliments is such a promoter of good feeling.

H. (*more stiffly*). I see I have been remiss. But I did not understand.

E. No, it is not yet time—but I have betrayed his confidence inadvertently. To-morrow you must congratulate me. To-morrow I shall tell you that I am engaged. Let me give you another cup.

H. (*rising*). No, one is enough. Once ought always to be enough! But it seems I am fated to have it twice! I know I am incoherent—but never mind! It's the tea!

E. (*playing with her teaspoon a little nervously*). And you have forgiven me?

H. I do not know that I have. But (*coldly*) whether I have or not is of course only a personal matter.

E. (*feebly*). Of course.

H. And so you are to tell me to-morrow that you are engaged? Might I ask you if, in taking this step, you were actuated by a wish to obtain my forgiveness ?

E. (*laughing*).   I expected you to ask mine—for being engaged to Mattie Montgomery.

H. (*sits*).   Suppose this afternoon you tell me about the—to be colloquial—the happy man.   And I will have some more tea.

E. (*looking into the sugar-bowl*).   Well, to tell the truth this afternoon—he doesn't happen—to be—colloquially—the happy man.

H. (*aside; walking about*).   So that note was written to-day.   I did not see the date.   It is not yet five o'clock, and it is not yet too late.   I shall gain nothing by getting rattled and making a fool of myself.   (*Aloud, coming back and holding out his cup, into which* ESTHER *drops sugar as they speak.*)   Have I then taken his place ?

E. (*gravely*).   No.   He is (*lump*) con-

servative (*lump*) in his (*lump*) tastes
(*lump*). He takes (*lump*) no sugar (*lump*)
at all (*lump*) in his.

H. (*who has been watching* ESTHER'S
*face, and not her fingers, sets down his
cup hastily*). Seven lumps *is* a little radi-
cal. Then you have forgotten all in four
years? (*Pacing the floor.*) Forgotten
what I, Esther, have been fool enough to
remember as if it had happened yester-
day! Who is it talks about woman's con-
stancy?

E. (*aside*). Not I. But I am very much
afraid I shall begin to. Has the tea gone
to my head too?

H. (*with much feeling*). The bitterest
lesson the four years have taught me,
Esther, is that one's earliest lessons are
never unlearned. They have been kinder
to you.

E. (*in a low tone*). Have they? Perhaps. They have taught us both, however, that it is not necessary to unlearn

them ; one can go on as if one had never studied—old lessons.

H. Or old letters ? (*Coming nearer and taking up the letter.*) But you did care for me enough to keep this letter—to read it over to-day—to give one thought to old happiness in the presence of new ?

E. (*recovering herself with an effort*). I thought enough of myself to keep it. It is a mistaken theory that a woman keeps old love-letters for the sake of the sender. She keeps them because they are flattering—because they—they sound nice. I have lots more.

H. (*offended*). And you were only weeding them out to-day ? Very well. That is enough. No further words are necessary.

E. Yes—so you said before (*glancing at letter*), or something very like it. (*Looking into the teapot.*) There is no more tea for us, and the lamp has gone out. (*Looking about.*) And no matches—unless you have one in your pocket.

H. (who has been thinking, moodily feels in all his pockets).   I am very sorry—but I cannot supply you with even the necessaries of life.

E. Never mind, I can light it from the fire.

H. (pushes the letters toward her). Make a lamplighter of one of these, and I will light it for you.

ESTHER *hesitates an instant, takes up one letter, and then the other.*

H. Oh, use mine.   It has failed to rekindle a passion, but it may do for a teakettle.   It may as well be reduced to ashes along with the rest of the poor little love-story.

ESTHER *turns her head a little away and slowly twists both letters into lamp-lighters.*

H. (aside). I shall let all my hopes burn in the flame with my letter.   If she uses that, I give her up.   I shall know she is not mine to give up.   I have come to the pass where folly is my only reason.

She is twisting Dr. Tennant's! But now she is twisting mine. (*She rises to go to the fire and he rises to do it for her.*)

E. I prefer to do it myself.

She returns with one burning, with which she lights the lamp, and lays the other down on the table. He takes it up eagerly.

H. So, Esther, you did not burn it, after all? (*Rising and coming toward her.*) You did not care that the last of it should go out in ashes?

E. (*speaking lightly*). It was not that so much, but I was afraid it was better suited for an—extinguisher. I think that was more what you meant it for.

HAROLD *goes back to his seat gloomily and tastes his tea.* ESTHER *plays with the tea-spoon—a pause.*

E. How do you like your tea?

H. It is a little—cloying.

E. (*rising and moving about the room*). A bad fault.

......

H. (*dryly*). But fortunately an uncommon one.

E. (*with feeling*).   I have made a great many mistakes in my life—suffered a great deal of unhappiness—because I have been afraid of being cloying. (*Aside.*) Am I mad, that I should tell him the foolish truth !

H. (*rising*).   I should say it was a fault to which you were not constitutionally inclined. (*Aside.*)   That sounds much firmer than I feel.

E. No, but on that very account people should have borne with me more than they have ! (*Still with feeling.*) Things might have been different.

H. (*going toward her*). Esther ! (*A bell.*)

E. (*hurriedly*). Never mind ! There is the door-bell ! Things are going to be different ! (*With a faint smile.*) I told you he did not like any sweet at all in his.

H. (*impetuously*).   And have I not had my full allowance of bitter ? It is time you began dispensing sweets—so let him stay away.

E. (*laughing nervously*).   But—but it wasn't my idea to get rid of him.

H. The plan is ready for your accept-ance.   You were going to tell me you were engaged to-morrow—tell him so to-day, instead !

E. (*glancing at clock*).   I cannot. His engagement was made with me a week ago.

H. And mine five years ago.   (*She hes-itates.*)   Besides, he is late—half an hour late.   What is it about a lover who is late ?   He has divided his time into more than " the thousandth part of a minute."

E. (*laughing*).   And are you not later —by four years ?

H. (*firmly*).   I am twenty-four hours ahead of time.

A knock.   Enter maid with a card.

E. Show him into the reception-room.

I will come in a moment. (*Exit maid.*) It is he, Harold. I must go.

H. (*taking her hands*). Esther, think one moment. Forget the four years. I have come a day too soon. I have swallowed two cups of tea and eight lumps of sugar and made a general ass of myself—but—I love you.

E. But—but this is so shameless! I thought I should have to say—something like that—to him.

H. (*coolly*). And I am in time to save you from so unfortunate a mistake. You had much better tell it to me.

E. But I must give him an answer.

H. Give me one first! Adopt my plan, it is so simple. Send word—or tell him, if you like—that you are engaged. But come back!

E. Indeed, he shall have his answer first. His right demands precedence at least. But (*opening the door*) I will come back.

H. To five years ago ?

E. Perhaps. (*Returns just as she is leaving the room.*) But, Harold, Harold, I thought an afternoon tea was so safe, or I should *never* have asked you.

H. And so did I—or I should never have come.

CURTAIN.

THE COMMONEST POS-
SIBLE STORY

BY BLISS PERRY

PHILANDER ATKINSON, bachelor of law and writer of light verse, sat one murky August evening in his hall-bedroom, with the gas turned low, wondering whether the night would be too hot for sleep. At a quarter before ten a loitering messenger-boy brought him a line from his friend Darnel: *Come around at once. Just back. The very greatest news.* Thereupon Atkinson discarded his smoking-jacket, reluctantly exchanged his slippers for shoes, and took the car down to

Twelfth Street, remembering meanwhile
that Darnel's brief vacation from the
Broadway Bank expired that day, and
speculating as to the nature of the great
news which the clerk had brought back
from Vermont. The lawyer was a Ver-
monter too, and it was this fact, as well
as a common literary ambition, that had
drawn the young fellows together at first,
long before Philander, on the strength of
having two triolets paid for, had moved up
to Thirty-first Street. Philander Atkinson liked Darnel, admired his feverish energy and his pluck, envied his acquaintance with books. He had always persisted
in thinking that Darnel's stories would
sell, if only some magazine would print
one for a starter; and he had patiently
listened to most of these stories, and to
some of them several times over. Yet
Darnel had never had any luck; had
never had even his deserts; and the sin-
cerity of his congratulations whenever

Atkinson's verses saw the light always caused Philander to feel a trifle awkward. He knew that the indefatigable clerk had two or three manuscripts " out "—out in the mails—when the vacation began, and as he turned in at Darnel's boarding-house he had almost persuaded himself that *The Æon* had accepted " Laki," his friend's Egyptian story. It was a long climb up to Darnel's room, and the writer of light verse mounted deliberately, being fat with overmuch sitting in his office chair. On the third floor the air was heavy with orange-flowers and Bonsilene roses, and a caterer was carrying away ice-boxes. A whimsical rhyme came into Philander's head, and he made a mental note of it. Just then Darnel appeared, leaning over the balustrade of the fourth-floor landing, his coat off, his collar visibly the worse for the railway journey, and an eager smile upon his thin, homely face.

" Hullo, D.," said Philander. " Here

I am.   Been having a wedding here?"
he added in a low voice, as he grasped
Darnel's hand.

"I believe so.   I'm just back.   Come
in, Phil.   You got my message?"

"Why else should I be here, old fellow?   Is it 'Laki,' sure?"

Without answering, Darnel led the way
into his tiny room. .His trunk lay upon
the floor, half-unpacked, the folding-bed
was down, for the better accommodation
of some of the trunk's contents, and the
desk in the corner, under the single jet of
gas, was covered with piles of finely torn
paper.   Darnel's manner, usually nervous
and somewhat conscious, betrayed a certain exhilaration, but he was under perfect self-control.

"'Laki?'" he said, seating himself in
his revolving chair and whirling around
to the desk, while Atkinson threw himself
upon the bed, "'Laki?'   Oh, I had forgotten.   It's probably here."   He pulled

over the mail accumulated during his absence. " Yes." He tore open the big envelope. " ' The editor of *The Æon* regrets to say,' etc. ; " and he tossed the printed slip, with the manuscript, into his waste-basket, with a laugh.

Atkinson's heart sank. Poor Darnel; it was not a cheerful welcome home. But Darnel was busied with his letters.

" And here are the others," he went on. " I thank the Lord none of them were accepted."

" What ! " exclaimed Philander, turning upon his elbow.

Darnel looked at him with a puzzling smile.

" That's why I sent for you," said he. " Phil, all that I've been writing here for three years is stuff, and I've only just found it out. I can do something different now."

Atkinson stared. Darnel had rarely talked about his own work, and then in a scarcely suppressed fever of excitement and anxiety. Many a time had Atkinson noticed his big hollow eyes turn darker, and his sallow face grow ashy, even in reading over with a shaking voice some of that same " stuff."

" I have learned the great secret," Darnel added, quietly.

" You have Aladdin's ring ? " said Atkinson. " Or are you in love ? "

" Both," replied Darnel. " It is the same thing."

Philander flung himself back upon the pillow, with a little laugh. " Go ahead, D."

" I have found her, and myself. Let me turn down the gas a little ; I see it hurts your eyes. I belong in the world now ; I am in the heart of it—I said to myself coming down the river this afternoon—in the heart of the world." He lingered over the words. " Phil," he exclaimed, suddenly, " all the time I was trying to write I was really trying to lift myself by the boot-straps. I was laboring to imagine things and people, and to get them on paper. It was all wrong. Do you remember that French poem you read me last winter, about the idol and the Eastern princess—how she lay on her couch sleeping—the night was hot—with the bronze idol gazing at her with its porphyry eyes, while her brown bosom rose and sank in her sleep, and the porphyry eyes kept staring at her — staring — but they never saw? Well, I believe my eyes have been like that. In ' Laki,' now, you know I wanted to describe the exact color of the stone in the quarry, and asked the Egyptologist up at the Museum to tell me what it was? He laughed at me. Very well. It was a dull-red stone, with bright-red streaks across it ; I saw the same thing in Troy this afternoon, when a hod-carrier fell five stories and they' picked him up from a pile of bricks."

"You're getting rather realistic," muttered Philander. Darnel was not looking at him, and went on unheeding.

"I have but to tell what I see. I have stopped imagining ; my head has ached— Phil, you don't know how it has ached— trying to imagine things. I am past that now ; if you only shut your eyes and look, it is all easy. Take that old Edda story that I tried to work up, about the fellow who fought all day long against his bride's father, and when night came the bride stole out and raised all the dead men on both sides, by magic, so that the next day, and every day, the battle raged on as before. I used to plan about the magic she used, and tried to invent a charm. Why, all she did was to pass over the battle-field at night, where the dead lay twisted in the frost, and while the wolves snarled around her and the spray from the fiord wet her cheek, she stooped to touch the dead men's wrists ; and they loosed their grip upon broken sword and split linden shield, their breath came again, soft and low like a baby's, and so they slept till the red dawn."

" Look here," said Atkinson, sitting up very straight, " you've been reading ' The Finest Story in the World,' and it has turned your head."

" Oh, the London clerk who was conscious of pre-existences, and forgot them all when he fell in love ? I could have told Rudyard Kipling better than that myself." Darnel gave an impatient whirl to the revolving chair.

" You mean you think you can," replied Atkinson, sharply.

" As you like." He spoke dreamily, and Atkinson dropped back on the pillow again, watching his friend as narrowly as the dim light would allow. Hard work and unearthly hours had told on Darnel ; he certainly seemed light-headed.

" Sickening heat—black frost—" he was

murmuring ; marching, stealing, fighting, toiling—joy, pain—the life of the race—is a man to grow unconscious of these things in the moment that he really enters the life of the race, that he feels himself a part of it? What do you think, Phil?"

"I think," was the slow reply, "that whatever has happened to you in Vermont has shaken you up pretty well, old fellow. They say that when someone asked Rachel how she could play *Phèdre* so devilishly well, she just opened her black Jewish eyes and said, ' I have seen her.' And I think, in the mood you're in now, you can see as far back as Rachel or anybody else. It's like being opium-drunk ; if you could keep so, and put on paper what you see, you could beat Kipling and all the rest of them. But you can't keep drunk, and you can't write prose or verse on love-delirium. It's been tried."

"Suppose Rachel had said, ' I *am* *Phèdre?*'"

Atkinson lifted his stout shoulders, laughing uneasily. " So much the worse. I should say, the less pre-existence of that sort the better. You might as well tell me the whole story, D. What is her name ? "

" In a moment. She loves me, Phil. She is waiting for me in her little house among the hills. I left her only this morning, and soon I shall go back and leave New York forever. I can write the story up there—the story I have dreamed of writing—for I shall always have the secret of it. I have but to shut my eyes and tell what I see ; and it is because she loves me. All the life of all the past— I can call that ' A Story of the Road.' Then there will be the future to write of —the men and women that are to come ; for we shall have children, Phil, and in them——"

" You're making rapid progress," ejaculated Philander.

" ——I shall know the story of the fut-

ure.   Even now I know it ; I do not sim-
ply foresee it, I see it.   Why not ' A
Story of the Goal ! '   For I belong to it—
do you not understand ?   Yet, after all,
what is that compared with the present ?
It shall be ' A Story of the March ! '
Look there ! "

He threw his eyes up to the ceiling,
which was brightened for an instant by
the headlight of an elevated train as it
rushed past.

" Do you know what that engineer was
really thinking of as he went by ?   That
would be story enough.   Or what was in
the heart of the bride to-night, down on
the   third   landing — you   smelled   the
orange-flowers as you came up ?   To feel
that your heart is in them, and theirs in
you——"

But Philander Atkinson was not listening to the lover's rhapsody.   He was
thinking of a certain summer when he,
too, had had strange fancies in his head ;

when his thoughts played backward and forward with swift certainty ; when he had grown suddenly conscious of great desires and deep affinities, and for a space of some three months he had dreamed of being something more than a mere verse-maker, a master of the file. Then—whether it was that she grew tired of him, or they both realized that some dull mistake had been made—it was all over. There was still in his drawer a package of manuscript he had written that summer ; in blank verse, none too noble a form for the high thoughts which then filled him ; in a queer new rhythm, too, the secret of whose beat he had caught at and then lost, for the lines read harshly to him now. He looked these things over occasionally, as a sort of awful example of himself to himself ; though he had gone so far as to borrow some of their imagery, not without a certain shame, to adorn his light verse. His card-house had fallen, but some of

the colored pasteboard was pretty enough
to be used again. Curiously, he found
that he could cut pasteboard into more
ingenious shapes than ever since his brief
experience in piling it ; fancy served him
better after imagination left him ; his triolets were admirably turned, and his luck
with the magazines began. Altogether it
had been an odd experience ; half those
crazy ideas of Darnel had been his two
years before, but he was quite over them
—yes, quite—and now it was D.'s turn.
He listened again to something that Darnel was murmuring.

"And she is an ordinary woman, one
would say ; a common woman. That is
the mystery and the glory of it. I do not
know that she is even beautiful. There
must be thousands of women like her ; I
can see it plainly enough, that there must
be thousands of women in the world like
her." There was a reverent hush in his
voice.

Atkinson choked back an exclamation.
Was D.'s head really turned ?   "A common woman "—" not know whether she is

beautiful ? "   A face rose before him, un-
like any face in all the world : eyes with
the blue of Ascutney, when you look at it
through ten miles of autumn haze ; hair

brown as the chestnut leaf in late October; mouth——

Philander trembled slightly, and rising to his feet, stood looking down at Darnel, haggardly. It was quite over, that experience of two summers before, but while it lasted he had at least never dreamed that there were thousands of women in the world like *her*.

"Sit down, Phil, I am almost through. A woman like other women, and the story, when I write it, a common story. It will be the commonest possible story; common as a rose, common as a child. I am going back to Vermont, where I was born, and where I have been born anew. There will be plenty of time for the story —years, and years, and years. I have only to close my eyes some day, and she will write down all I tell her, and I shall call the story hers and mine."

But Atkinson still stood, his hands in his pockets, his heavy figure stooping, the lines hardening in his face, while he watched the rapt gaze of Darnel, and drearily reflected how strange it was that a woman should open all the gates of the wonder-world to one man's imagination, and that some other woman should close those secret gates, quietly, inexorably, upon that man's friend.

"Wait," said Darnel. "Must you go back to your triolets? Let me show you her picture first." He turned the gas up to its fullest height, and held out a photograph.

It was the same woman.

THE END OF THE BEGIN-NING

By George A. Hibbard

CITY OF NEW YORK,
April 10, 1887.

DEAR SIR: It is with some hesitation
that I venture to trespass upon your val-
uable time, knowing as I do that the
demands of clients, of constituents, of

friends, are so exacting. Still, as what I
am about to ask relates to a matter lying
very near my heart, I hope you will forgive me. A young man in whom, in spite
of the usual extravagances and follies of
youth, I discern some promise, and whom
I hope, for his own sake and from my
friendship for his excellent father, dead
long ago, to see occupying a respectable
position in the community, has, with the
heedlessness peculiar to his age, involved
himself in certain difficulties which, although at present of a sufficiently distress-
ing nature, may, I hope, be satisfactorily
overcome. Knowing so well your distinguished abilities, ripe judgment, and
great experience, I can think of no one to
whom I can, in this critical period of his
life, more confidently send him for counsel, instruction, and aid, and I according-
ly commend him to you, trusting to our
old friendship to account for and excuse
my somewhat unusual act. Though what
I ask of you is something not usually re-
quired of a lawyer, I think you will understand my reason for thus troubling you.
No one can have a more thorough knowl-

edge of the world than an old practitioner like yourself, and what you may say must fall upon the ears of youth with weighty authority. Talk to him as you would to your son, if you had one, not as to a client, and I will be inexpressibly indebted to you, for I know you will lead him to appreciate the serious realities of life, which, at present, he is so disposed to disregard.

I need only add that he is a young man of some fortune, and, certainly, by birth worthy of much consideration. He will call upon you in person and himself explain his present embarrassments.

I remain, now as always,

Your obedient servant,

RICHARD BEVINGTON.

THE HON. JACOB MASKELYNE,
    Counsellor at law,
        Number—William Street,
            City of New York.

This was the letter that the Honorable Jacob Maskelyne read, reread, and read yet again. Indeed, not content with its repeated perusal, he turned it this way and that, looked at it upside and down, and finally, laying it upon the table, he held up its envelope in curious study, as people so often do when thus perplexed. It bore the common, dull-red two-cent stamp and was post-marked the day before. Both it and the letter were apparently as much matters of the every-day world as a jostle on the side-walk. Nevertheless, the old lawyer was more than puzzled—more than puzzled, although he, of all men in the great, wide-awake city, would in popular opinion have been thought perhaps the very last to be thus at fault. If millstones were to be worn as monocles—if there was any seeing what the future might bring forth—the chances of a project, the risks of rise or fall in a stock, the hazards of a corner in a staple, the prospects of a party or of a partisan, Jacob Maskelyne would be regarded as the man of men for the work.

But, under the circumstances, even to him
this letter was more than perplexing.
Here, on this spring morning, with floods
of well-authenticated sunshine pouring
into every nook and corner, dissipating
every mystery of shadow and, it might
seem, every shadow of mystery—here, in
his office, bricked in by the unimagina-
tive octavos of the law—those hide-bound
volumes, heavy literature of all things
most amazingly matter of fact ; here, in
the eighteen hundred and eighty-seventh
year of the Christian era, in the one hundred and eleventh year of the Republic,
he had received a letter from his old
guardian, whom, when he himself was not
more than twenty, he remembered walking about a feeble old man with many
an almost Revolutionary peculiarity in
speech and manner, and whose funeral
he, with the heads and scions of most of
the first families of the town, had attend-
ed full twenty-five years ago.   It certainly

was enough to bewilder anyone He
again took up the letter. It was unques-

tionably in old Bevington's best style, courtly enough, but a trifle pompous. Had it not been for its true tone he would undoubtedly have thought the thing a hoax and immediately have dismissed it from his mind. He touched a hand-bell, and in response a young man—a very prosaic young man—over whose black clothes the gray of age had begun to gather, appeared.

" Bring me the letters received of the year eighteen sixty — letter B," said the lawyer, sharply.

That was the year in which his father's estate had been finally settled, and he knew that there would be many examples of his guardian's handwriting in the correspondence of that time.

The clerk soon returned with a tin case, and laid it on the table. Mr. Maskelyne took one from among the many papers therein, and, striking it sharply against the arm of his chair, to scatter the dust

that invests all things in the garment the
outfitter Time warrants such a perfect fit,
he spread it out beside the letter he had
just read with such blank wonder.

" Identically the same," he muttered.
" No other man ever made an *e* like
that."

The clerk had vanished and the lawyer
was again alone.

He glanced once more at the mysterious
missive, and then, with the purposeless-
ness of abstraction, he rose and went to
the window.   Nothing caught his eye but
the sign-bedecked front of the opposite
building and one small patch of blue sky
—near, gritty, limestone fact and a far-
away something without confine. Still,
amazed as he was the contagious joy of
the time sensibly affected him.

The sparrows, quarrelsome gamins of
the air, for the time reformed by honest
labor into respectable artisans, upon an
opposite entablature, in garrulous amity

plied their small, nest-
making joinery. The
sunlight falling through
a haze of wires, wrought

into something bright
with its own glow a tuft
of grass which clumped
its spears in its fortalice,
taken in assault, on the

opposite frieze. Of even these small
things, and of much more, Mr. Maskelyne was partially conscious. But the letter! Clear-sighted as he was, he knew
but little—so forthright was his look, so
fixed toward mere gain—of the wonderful country which lies beneath every man's
nose, less even of the vanishing tracts
which retrospection sometimes sees over
either shoulder. But the letter! It peo-
pled his vision with things long gone. It
brought into view old Bevington—"Dick
Bevington," as he was called to the last
day of his life—and a nickname at fifty
indicates much of character; brought up
before him Dick Bevington as he was before age had stiffened his easy but digni-
fied carriage or taught his once polished
but positive utterance to veer and haul in
sudden change; brought up old Bevington, as he himself, in childhood, had seen
him, stately but debonair, the perfection
of aristocratic exclusiveness, affable, how-

ever, in the genial kindliness of a kind-
hearted man secure in every position—a
genuine Knickerbocker in every practice
and in every principle—a well-born, well-
bred gentleman.   And that once active
and once ebullient life had long ago gone
out !   It almost seemed that such vitality,
so held in self-contained management, so
wisely put forth, so well invested, so to
speak, should have lasted forever.   But
now there was nothing left to bring him to
mind but a portrait in the rooms of the
Historical Society, or a name in the list of
directors when the history of some bank
was given, or in the pamphlet in which
the story of some charitable institution
was told from the beginning—really there
was nothing more than this to recall Dick
Bevington, foremost among the city's fa-
thers, the leader of the *ton*.   When he
had last seen his guardian he had thought
him of patriarchal age.   And was not he
himself now nearly as old ?   In spite of

the blithesome aspects of the morning, Jacob Maskelyne turned away from the window with an unwonted weight at his heart and a new wrinkle on his brow. The whole world seemed to be going from him, losing charm and significance in a sort of blurring dissatisfaction, as upon a globe, when swiftly turned, lines of longitude and of latitude, and even continents and seas, vanish from sight, and all because his own life suddenly seemed but vexed nothingness. He had not even mellowed into age as had Bevington. He was as sharp and as rough-edged as an Indian's flint arrow-head, and he knew it.

He seated himself at his table. Automatically he was about to take up the first of several bundles of law-papers, when he was startled by the entrance of the clerk. He leaned back in his chair, and his re-awakened wonder grew the more when a card was placed before him upon which was written, in a dashing hand, " From Mr. Bevington."

" A gentleman to see you," said the clerk.

" What does he look like ? " asked Mr. Maskelyne, suspiciously.

" Nobody I ever saw before," answered the clerk ; " and he seems rather strange about his clothes," he added, in a rather doubtful, tentative manner.

" Let him come in," said Mr. Maskelyne, after a moment's pause.

The door had hardly closed upon the vanishing messenger when it again swung upon its hinges, and a new figure stood in relief against the clearer light from without. In his eagerness to see of what nature a being so introduced might be, Mr. Maskelyne turned his chair completely around, and silently gazed at the new-comer as he entered. His eyes fell upon a slim, graceful young man dressed in the mode of at least forty-five years ago—a mode not without its own good tone undoubtedly, but with a tendency toward gorgeousness which an exquisite of these days of as-

sertive unobtrusiveness might think almost vulgar. His whole attire was touched in every detail with that nameless something which really makes the consummate result unattainable by any not born to such excellence; but in the bright intelligence shining in his dark eyes and the clear intellectual lines of his face, even

Maskelyne could see that if he had given much thought to his dress it was only from a proper self-respect, and not because dress was the ultimate or the best expression of what he was. Few could look into the luminous countenance and not feel a glow of sudden sympathy with the high aspirations, the pure disinterestedness, the clear intellect, that lit up and strengthened his features. Even the old lawyer, disciplined as he was by years of hard experience to disregard all such misleading impulses, felt his heart warm toward the young man.

"I hope," said the new-comer, with a smile so pleasant, so ingenuous, so confiding, that all Maskelyne's ideas of deception—had he had time to recognize them in the moment before a strange, unquestioning acquiescence took complete possession of him—were at once dissipated, "that I do not intrude too greatly on your time."

Won really in spite of himself by the appearance of his visitor, the famous counsellor waved his hand toward a chair.

" I suppose," continued the stranger, with an almost boyish sweetness, as he seated himself, " that Mr. Bevington has already told you why I am here."

Mr. Maskelyne might very well have answered that Mr. Bevington was hardly to be looked to for any information on any subject, but he did not—the wonderful circumstances of the interview had been so driven from his mind by the potent charm of the young man's personality.

" Mr." — and he paused as if waiting for enlightenment as to the name of the stranger.

" I'm in a devil of a scrape," continued the young man, apparently imagining that the letter had made all necessary explanations, and mentioning the devil as though he was an every-day acquaintance, a pleasant fellow whom he had just left at the door awaiting his return.

" Ah ! " murmured the lawyer.

" I did not wish to see you," continued the other, his singularly trustful smile breaking again over lip and cheek.

" Indeed," said Maskelyne, his wits and perceptions in most confusing entanglement.

" No," went on the unaccountable visitor. " I supposed that you would give me what the world calls good advice. But I don't want that. I want to hear something better."

He laughed aloud in such a joyous, cheery fashion that the old lawyer even smiled.

" You don't think I am a good man to come to for bad advice ? " he said.

" The last in the world. I don't suppose that you ever did a foolish thing in your life."

" And therefore am perhaps less com-

petent to advise others who have," replied Maskelyne, half heedlessly, for his
thoughts were slowly turning in a new
direction. The more he looked the more
the eager, spirited face seemed familiar.
He had certainly seen the young fellow
before, but where ? It seemed to him
that he could certainly remember in a
moment, if he only had time to think.

" Mr. Bevington——"

" Pardon me," interrupted Maskelyne,
in a significant tone, " you said Mr. Bevington ? "

" Certainly," said the stranger, suddenly looking up in evident surprise.
" Didn't he write ? "

" I have received a letter," said the
old lawyer, cautiously.

He was on the point of making some
further inquiries, but the impulse came
to nothing. The former feeling of ac-
quiescent but expectant apathy again
possessed him ; indeed, he had never

been much in the habit of asking questions. He knew that he often learned more than was suspected even, by letting people talk on in their own way.

" In the first place," and he paused a moment—"I am very much in debt." The young man spoke as he might of taking a cold asleep in the open air—as if he had been exposed to debt and had caught it.

The first look of sadness rose and deepened over his face as he shook his head dejectedly.

" But I'll get over it—'Time and I.' Don't you rather like the astute old king after all, Mr. Maskelyne ? "

" By your own exertions ? " asked the lawyer, dryly, and evading the question.

" I write a little," replied the impenitent, modestly. " I have even heard of people who admired some of my verses."

" You have no other occupation ? "

Old Maskelyne was asking enough

questions now. Indeed, under the magic of the stranger's manner he had quite forgotten himself, his usual caution, and even the exceptional manner in which his companion had been introduced to him.

" Yes," the other admitted, " I am a lawyer."

" Don't you think," said the older man, answering almost instinctively, " that on the whole you might find the employments of the law more remunerative than the calling of a—poet ? "

" Mr. Maskelyne, I sometimes think that the world really believes in the sort of thing underlying your question—that there is wisdom in what it so complacently repeats as indisputable. And I am sent here phrase-gathering—to carry off small packages of words put up in little flat, portable sentences, alteratives ready for daily use. But there are gains you cannot invest in lands and stocks—columns with statues at the top as well as

columns whose sums are at the bottom.
Wasn't ' Le Barbier ' a better investment
than any in Roderigue Hortales et Cie.,
and what could John Ballantyne & Co.
show beside ' Guy Mannering ? ' If the
world says what it does, it mustn't do as
it does. It's inconsistent. Who will undertake to strike the balance between
fame and fortune ; what mathematician
will undertake to say that x, the unknown
quantity of fame, does not equal the
dollar-mark ? " Then he added, after a

moment's p a u s e ,
" M r . Maskelyne,
don't you think it is
true that

" ' One crowded hour of
glorious life,
Is worth a world with-
out a name,'—

don't you really ? "

It was hard to re-
sist such enthusiasm,

such unquestioning certainty. The old lawyer did not even smile as he lay back in his chair, a new life shooting through every nerve, his gaze fixed on the flushing face of the young man.

" And the consciousness of best employing the best that is in you," he continued. " Who dare shorten the reach or blunt the nicety of man's wit, make purblind the imagination, stiffen the cunning hand ? Tell men that in some Indian sea, fathoms deep, lie hid forever Spanish galleons in which doubloons and moidores, as when honey more than fills the comb, almost drip from their sacks, and you will see in their sudden thoughtfulness how quickly they appreciate such loss ; tell them, if you can, what, through poverty, erring endeavor, uncongenial occupation, the world with each year loses in intellectual riches, and they will stand heedless."

Speaking with the incomparable confi-

dence of youth, its own glorious nonsense,
the young man's voice sent old Maskelyne's blood hastening through his veins
in almost audible pulsations.

" What if I do not wish great wealth,"
the speaker continued, " must I be made
to have it ? I want but little. Give me
food, clothing, habitation, sufficient that
my eyes may see the delights this world
has to show, that my ears may catch the
whispered harmonies of all things beautiful, gladden me with the radiance of common joy, and that's all I want. Who is
unreasonable when what he wants is all
he wants ? Are the worldly so insecure
that, as the frightened kings sought to
still beneath their tread the first throb of
the French Revolution, they must stamp
out the first symptom of revolt against
the almighty dollar ?

" 'Chi si diverte di poco, è ricco di molto.'

Mr. Maskelyne, must I eat when I am

only thirsty, drink when I am only hungry?"

He paused, and glanced triumphantly at the old man. He felt in some secret, instinctive way that he was gaining ground. A squadron of fauns had charged from amid the vine-leaves, and the legion upon the highway was in rout. Fine sense was victorious for the moment over common sense.

"I think," said Maskelyne, at last, and with a strange, sad, patient air, unwearied, however, by the young man's dithyrambic, sometimes almost incoherent speech, "I think I cannot attempt to advise you. Having discarded the wisdom of ages, what heed will you give the wisdom of age?"

A cloud seemed to cast its shadow over the other's face. Could it be that, lost in himself, he had spoken almost in presumptuous disrespect to a man so distinguished, to a man whom he honored

and whom he felt that he could even
like ?

" If I speak strongly," he said, " it is
because I feel strongly. If I did not feel
strongly I would not attempt to with-
stand the amount of testimony against
me."

" Might I ask," said Maskelyne, gently,
in his inexplicable sympathy with the
young fellow, " why, if you feel such confidence in all you say, you do not, without
hesitation, enter on a life in accordance
with your convictions ? "

At last there was hesitation in the young
stranger's manner. He turned his hat
nervously in his hand, and sat silent for a
moment.

" You see," he began, paused, and began again—" You see, if I were alone it
would be one thing. But I'm not—not at
all alone," he added, evidently gaining
confidence.

" Ah ! " exclaimed the old lawyer, a

sudden gleam of new intelligence shining in his dull, weary old eyes.

"And how am I to get married, Mr. Maskelyne?"

"The lady does not approve of your— poetic aspirations?"

"Not approve!" cried the young fellow, eagerly; "she has made me promise that I will give nothing up, that I will refuse all Mr. Bevington has arranged for me. You can't tell how inspiring our misery is. And our courage,—a young Froissart must be our chronicler, sir. We take our sorrows gladly."

"And may I ask——"

"Anything, anything," interrupted the young man, gayly. "I'm sent here to be talked out of what they may call my folly. You see I can't be talked out of it. Don't that prove that it is no folly?"

"You seem," said Maskelyne, dryly, "to have settled it between you — you and she."

" Settled it ! We did not need help
about that. It's the unsettling.   There
comes a time when friends are the worst
enemies. You know that, Mr. Maskelyne ? "

The old lawyer paused.   " Indeed I
do," he said at last, and the sneer stealing
over the outlines of his face slunk away before the look of regret that came swiftly on.
Almost in embarrassment, with nervous
hand, he shuffled the papers on his table.

Far back in the past, when his eyes
were not yet dimmed by the dust blown
from law-books, nor his ears deadened by
the stridulent clamor of litigation before
his life had gone in attempts at

" Mastering the lawless science of our law,"

or he had lost himself in

" That codeless myriad of precedent,
    That wilderness of single instances ; "

when he, too, dwelt in that other-world
of the young, forgotten by everyone but

himself, but, although hardly ever remembered, never forgotten by him—not one grain of its golden sand, not one drop of its honey-dew, not one tremor of its slightest thrill—then even he had had his romance.   The freshness of the early spring morning, the airy brightness of his young visitor, himself no bad exponent of the day, the awe-footed shadow which, with almost unrecognized obtrusion, skirts the border where the ripened grain fills the field of life and nods to the ready sickle—was it something of such kind, or was it the simple story of which he had had such telling intimation, that brought it all up in memory's half-tender glow ? He, too, had once been in love.   He, too, had written verses to his inamorata.   He remembered it all now, with a smile of mingled pity and contempt.   It needed no ransacking of the brain now to quicken into full view his own " It might have been "—to people once more the mystic world whose first

paradise is rich in the slight garniture of
glances and sighs and smiles and tears.
Lost in himself, the old man forgot his
visitor.

" You are very young," he said at last,
absently.

" Twenty-three," was the answer.

" And she ? "

" Eighteen."

It was strange, but he, too, had been
twenty-three and she eighteen when the
end came in that glimmering, gleaming
past.   He remembered, and how strange
the recollection seemed, taking her some
flowers and some slight silver gift—a poor,
inexpensive thing ; she would let him give
no more because he, too, was in debt—on
her birthday.   And now, with strange re-
vulsion, he hardened almost into his habitual self, and grimly thought that it all
was youthful nonsense, and that all such
follies were very much alike.   Had he
spoken, he would have been guilty of

one of those faults often packed with error, an apothegm — he would have said that we only become original, even in our folly, as age gives us character.

" We could be so happy with so little," said the youthful lover.

The old man started. These were his own words many, many years ago ; his very words to his guardian when the final appeal was made by old Bevington to what he called his better judgment so very, very long ago, in the dark, stately house upon Second Avenue.

" So very little," repeated the young man. " I have always said," he continued, as pleased with the conceit as if it had never before glittered in the song of finches of his feather, " that we should have gold enough in her hair."

" And is her hair golden ? " asked Maskelyne, and, startled by the sound of such words dropped from the lips of the distinguished counsel for many a soulless corporation and many as soulless a man, he added, hurriedly, " light."   And then the old lawyer remembered that he too, had a lock of hair that he had not sent back when he returned her letters and her

picture.   How bright it was!   What had
become of it ?   Where was it ?   In what
pigeon-hole, what secret drawer ?   He
could not for the moment remember.   He
looked out of the window.   How bright
the sunshine was ! How empty the world !
It seemed to build up its vacancy around
him as a wall.

" And she, of course, has no money ? "
he said, turning again.

" None."

He had been sure of it.   He rose and
went to the window.   The joyful attributes
of the morning were there, but they were
no longer joyful to him.   The light fell in
the same broad flood, still promising the
glory of summer, the ripened harvest, but
there was no promise for him.   The sparrows preluded still the full-voiced singers
of the year, when leaves are heavy with
the dust and brooks run dry, but he heard
only a quick, petulant twitter.   A sort of
dull despondency suddenly settled upon

him. He forgot his visitor, and even time and place. Amid the glimmering lights and shaking shadows of the past he sought a vision, as at twilight one seeks in some deserted corridor a statue which would seem to have so taken into its grain the last rays of the already sunken sun that the marble glows in the gathering darkness with a radiance not its own.

The young man grew impatient as the revery was prolonged. He stirred uneasily. The old lawyer turned and looked curiously at him. Of course, of course! Was a man to be changed, the bone of what he was to have its marrow drawn, the fibre of every muscle to be untwisted, by this nonsense of a boy? Of course old Bevington was right—and for the moment he did not remember that Bevington was dead—in sending the young fool to such a cool old hand as himself. But if Bevington had known what a turbulence of disappointment, discontent, and revolt had risen, and poured in strength-gathering torrent, even at that instant, through his heart, would he not have kept his young charge away? He would talk to him—certainly he would—pave his way for him, perhaps, as with flagstones of wisdom. Perhaps—and then he thought with grim satisfaction of what Bevington might think should he learn that he recognized that there were other paths than those edged by a curbstone.

"You have been sent to me," he said, very seriously, coming from the window and leaning with both hands on the table, "for advice and admonition. I will give my lesson in sternest characters. I will teach by example, but I may not teach what you were sent here to learn. When I was young as you—do not start, I was young once," and he spoke with infinite sadness, "I loved as you love, and, as with you, love was returned. They who called themselves my friends strove, with

what they called reason, to tear me from what they called my folly. My folly! It was the wisdom that it takes all that is blent into humanity, at supremest moments, to attain ; their reason, the fatuous folly only enough to give habitual stir to an earth-beclotted brain! I yielded, as you have not yielded. I killed out even the natural impulses of my nature. Gradually almost new instincts came, desire for delight sank into appetite for gain, hope for the joy of higher existence was lost in the ambition for mere advancement. I wrought out in myself that fearful piece of handiwork whose every effort is but to grasp the worthless handful man can only wrest from the mere world. I lost, and I have not won. I was a man and I am only a lawyer, and to him you have been sent for advice. I can find no precedent better, no authority more weighty for your guidance than my own life. Such strength as enabled me to

work such a change will also enable you
to make yourself a new being, to accom-
plish self-overthrow, to bring you to what I
am—a man rich, successful, courted, re-
vered—most miserable. He who has so
won, so lost, stands alone or he would not
so win. Choose rather the close companionship of worldly defeat, if it must be, and
I say to you in the rapture of your youth,
clay plastic to the moment's touch, hold
to yourself, and believe that no fame, no
power, no wealth, can compensate for a
contentious life, an empty heart, a deso-
late old age. If I were you——"

He did not finish. Slowly the young
stranger rose to his full height, every lin-
eament of his face clear in cold light. His
whole aspect was one of steadfast com-
mand.

"Stop!" he cried, in a stern tone. "I
am yourself. No ghost ·walks save that
which is what a man might have been.
We throng the world. Beside everyone

through life moves the image of a past
potentiality, the thing he could have become had he held along another course.
I am what you were, the promise of what
you might have been.   For forty years I
have walked by your side.   I have touched
you and you have shuddered, I have
chilled you and you have shrunk from me.
Your nature has so grown athwart, all impulse has been so long gone, all that soft-
ens or ennobles so thrown off that, in almost final self-assertion, what you really
were or might have been stands by your
side and bids you measure stature with
itself.   Your life has entered upon its win-
try days, but sunlight is sunshine even in
December and in youth."

The old lawyer, almost shuddering,
stepped back with repelling gesture.   He
passed his hand quickly across his eyes,
and then, as if his heart had beat recall,
summoning back every retreating force in
quick rally, compelled but not unwilling,

he turned in combative instinct to meet
the stranger face to face, nature to nature,
turned—and found himself alone.

Once more the clerk opened the door.

"Eleven o'clock, sir," he said, "and
you know the General Term this morning——"

"You saw the gentleman who just went
out?" asked the lawyer.

"I, sir," answered the man; "I saw no
one go out."

"No one?"

"No one."

"You certainly brought me a card and
showed a young gentleman in a few minutes ago?"

"I, sir!" repeated the clerk. "I
brought in a card and showed a young
gentleman in! Aren't you well this morning, sir?"

"That will do," said Maskelyne, stern-
ly.

As soon as he was again alone he

stepped to the table. The card and the
letter were gone. And still he knew he
had not been dreaming. A man swung
high in the air was busy painting a sign
upon a building not far away, and he was
conscious that all through the strange interview he had watched him at work. He
had seen him finish one letter and then
another, and now if he found him adding
the final consonant he would be assured
that he could not have been asleep. He
looked up and found that he was right.
The man had just made the heavy shaded
side and was busy putting the little fin-
ishing line at the bottom of the letter.

Two men—one of rotund middle age,
the other younger but yet not young—
came down the steps of the Union Club
one day a few weeks later. They met
an old man rounding the corner of the
Avenue.

" See what you would come to if you
had your own way," said the elder of the
two.   " There's old Maskelyne.   He's
got everything you're making yourself
wretched to get.   Do you want to be like
him ? "

" No," said the other.   " Then you
haven't heard ? "

" Heard what ? "

" He's a changed man, all within a
month."

" Has his brain or his heart soft-
ened ? "

" As you look at life," said the younger.
" He has sent for that clever, improvident,
gracefully graceless good-fellow of a good-
for-nothing, his nephew, him and his
pretty-handed, big-eyed wife—he hadn't
seen either of them since they ran away
and were married—sent for them and put
them in his great, old house and—didn't
you hear Maceration growling about the
luck some people have just before we

left? He says the nephew will have all the old man's property."

"What's the world coming to?" said the senior, "or what is coming to the world?"

A PURITAN INGÉNUE

By John Seymour Wood

I.

THE Archibald house, on West Forty-
— Street, was of the character described
as a " modernized front."   A handsome
arch in rough stone surmounted the front-
door, which was done in polished oak and
plate-glass.   The stoop was on a level
with the sidewalk ; a richly carved bow-
window jutted out from the second story.
" No. 41," in old iron open work, formed

a pretty grating above the door. There was, in fact, nothing which would lead an ordinary person to conceive of the house as given over to boarders, except, possibly, the sign,

---

TO LET, FURNISHED.

---

which was posted conspicuously below the first-story window, and at an angle which enabled him that ran to read.

Old Mr. Archibald's death, the autumn before, had left his widow rather poorer than she anticipated. He was a great collector of pretty things. His taste was exquisite, and he had gratified it by filling his house with a variety of *bric-à-brac*, pictures, statuary, and old furniture, which made it a centre of attraction to many of the old gentleman's artistic friends. Mrs. Archibald, loath to dispose of her husband's art collections, determined to let the house, as it stood, " at an exorbitant figure, to a very rich tenant without children " Under these terms, on her departure for Europe, her agent was entrusted with the house, and her son Jerome, when he saw her off on the steamer, received a parting injunction, " Be sure and see that they have no children." Jerome Archibald saw his mother and sisters depart—in no very enviable frame of mind ; but he was a good son, and he resolved to forego Newport, if it would tend to dispose of the house as his mother wished, and add to her diminished income.

His mother and sisters sailed in May. It was now July, and very warm and disagreeable. As the "heated term" set in, he began to think it too bad, you know, of mamma and the girls to remain abroad for three whole years. It was positively absurd. What was he to do? After the house was let—where was he

to go? By Jove, he felt deuced lonely,
don't you know! It was especially trying
for a sensitive man to go in and out of a
house with a great placard on it, "To
Let, Furnished," but it was a deal more
trying to have people come and want
board. Yes, actually, two ladies came
one morning and wanted to know if they
could see the landlord. It was positively
ridiculous! His agent was a clevah fellow, but even he gave up hope of letting
the house until fall. Hadn't he better
run down to Newport? He got a letter
from Dick Trellis that morning, and they
really didn't see how they were going to
get on without him in the polo matches.
It put him in a fuming fury. He had
never stayed late in the city in summer
before. How infernally hot it was—and
nahsty—don't you know! His collars
were in a perpetual state of wilt—they
never wilted at Newport. Then everybody was not only out of town, having a

good time somewhere, but they had a provoking way now of ostentatiously boarding up their front-doors—yes—and their windows, too—which made it doubly disagreeable for those who had to remain. It was bad enough to see the blinds drawn down, but boxing up their stonework and planking up their front-doors caused Mr. Jerome Archibald unutterable pangs. Then they thought it was a boarding-house !

They were coming again in the afternoon, at four. There were two of them —ladies. In his rather depressing and solitary occupation of living alone in his house, with one solemn apoplectic cook and one chalk-faced maid, in order to exhibit it to that endless raft of females with " permits," who universally condemned or " damned with faint praise " his father's exquisite taste in rugs and furniture, Mr. Jerome Archibald had to-day admitted to himself a distinct pleasure in showing " Miss Perkins " and her niece (whose name did not happen at the time to be mentioned) over the house, and pointing out in his quiet way its excellences.

They saw the sign, they said, and so made bold to enter. Evidently Miss Perkins was a prim, thin, tall, spectacled, New England old maid. She had the delicate air and manner of a lady. A lady faded, perhaps, and unused to a larger social area than that surrounding her native village green. She had also the timid manner of hesitancy of New England spinsters — hesitancy concerning everything except questions of casuistry and religion—and seemed, in what she did, to be spurred on from behind by the niece, who was, on the whole, as Mr. Jerome Archibald told a friend at the club later, " quite extraordinary."

In the first place, as he said, the niece was undeniably beautiful.

"She wore rawther an odd street dress," he said, "made up in the country somewhere, by a seamstress who gathered her crude notions of the prevailing fashions from some prevaricating ladies' journal, and her hat was something positively ridiculous—but her *face!*" The fastidious Mr. Jerome Archibald at once conceded to it a certain patrician quality of elegance. It denoted pure blood and pure breeding, somewhere up among Vermont hills or Maine forests. A long line of "intelligent ancestors," perhaps. It was fine, and—beautiful. The forehead high, nose straight, the large eyes gray, the mouth and chin sweet, and yet quite determined. When he showed them a large room at the rear, on the second story, facing the north, the niece had observed, with a lofty air—mind, the room was literally crammed with the most costly *bric-à-brac*—"I think this will suit me very well, aunt dear, on account of the light."

He noticed in her unfashionable dress a certain artistic sense of freedom, a *soupçon* of colored ribbon here and there, and he concluded that she was all the more interesting, as an artist, in that she so quietly accepted the elegancies around her. She gave an unconscious sigh over a small glass-covered "Woodland Scene," by Duprez. Mr. Jerome Archibald noticed it, and inwardly smiled, delighted.

Perhaps the niece captivated him the more by her silent appreciation of some things he himself admired exceedingly. It was odd that she seemed always to choose *his* favorites. There was nothing said as to the rent, the size of the house, the lot, the plumbing. He spent an hour showing his etchings alone, and in the afternoon, at four, they were coming again, " to decide."

II.

Of course Mr. Jerome Archibald must have been an extremely susceptible young man to have fallen in love at first sight with a strange young woman, who had come to look at his house with a view to renting. But he was—"rawther down and depressed." The usual summer malaria had set in. The usual excavations in the streets were going on—they were digging with "really extraordinary energy" that summer—the pavements were up on all the Fortieth streets. Fifth Avenue presented the appearance of a huge empty canal. It was something more, this presidential year, than the perennial laying down and taking up of pipes. " He was really ripe for *une grande affaire du cœur*," said one of his club friends, he was getting so lonesome. He *did* fall quite entirely in love, precipitately, unquestionably, in spite of the fact that they took the house for a boarding-place! They asked to hire but one room only.

When they arrived, at 4 P. M., they sat a few moments in the reception-room, while the chalk-faced, alert maid announced them to Archibald in the room above. Miss Perkins folded her faded, gloved hands in her lap and sat up on the sofa stiffly. They had looked at ever so many houses, and they had come back to No. 41 with instinctive preference.

" I don't think one room would be so very expensive," said Miss Perkins. " He could put up two beds easily in that north room, and the room we saw on Thirty-fourth Street was only twelve dollars—what do you think, Elvira ? "

" I think twelve dollars is altogether too high," said the niece, looking up from a delicate little Elzevir she was holding. " I think he wants to let the rooms very much ; none of them seem to be taken. Remember it is midsummer, aunt dear."

There was a little pause.

"Of course he will prefer having *nice* people. It will be a great help to your art, Elvira—you can study at great advantage. There are so many pictures for you to copy. I think your father would say it was a 'lucky find.' If you will persist in your art, why, I think we are very fortunate."

"You are always ready to sneer at my art, Aunt Perkins." And she gave a peculiar laugh.

"It is something that has come up since my day," she replied, glancing about over the pictures and the rare editions on the table. "I was brought up to plain living. But I guess if we can get it all for twelve dollars we ought to be satisfied. It's a pleasant change to see the city. It's pleasant to see these ornaments. Yes, I don't blame art so much as your father does, Elvira, and I don't believe *he* would blame it if he knew we could have so much of it for twelve dollars."

"Father secretly admires it as much as I do," said the niece; "only he likes to talk."

Just then Mr. Jerome Archibald entered. He was faultlessly dressed in half-mourning for his father. Indeed, he had dressed himself with exceeding care, being desirous, he frankly admitted to himself, of making an impression. He bowed graciously, and took Elvira's extended gloved hand, which, as she offered it, he held a moment. "Have you decided?" he asked.

They had explained, when they left in the morning, that they should want only one room, and he tacitly inferred that they would require board. He received a dreadful shock, but made up his mind that the charming niece would prove the

more charming on closer acquaintance,
and he deliberately decided to keep both
the gentle New Englanders under his
roof for a time, if he could! The more
he thought of the plan, the more interesting the situation became to him. He
fairly dreaded, at last, lest they should
find their way into a remote boarding-
house in some cheap quarter of the city,
where it would be quite impossible for
him to follow them. He gravely announced to the astonished maid that
he had determined to let out the rooms
to the ladies, who, he pretended for
her benefit, were old acquaintances.
When they were announced he was
scarcely able to conceal his pleasure.
Mr. Jerome Archibald had fallen in
love.

"We have decided to take one room,"
said Elvira, "if we can agree upon the
price; and we wish to know the price of
board——"

"We shan't want much to eat," put in Miss Perkins, with a nervous twitch.

Archibald admirably concealed a smile. His long mustache aided him a good deal in doing this. He was still standing, and he put his hand to his lips: "I think we shall agree very easily upon the price," he said.

Miss Perkins again twitched a little. "We thought twelve dollars—room and board——" she said, leaving the sentence half finished, while Elvira looked up at him, expectantly.

"My dear ladies, I should not think of charging more than ten. You are strangers in the city, and I would not impose upon you for the world. It happens that this is the dull season——"

"So we thought," said Miss Perkins, "and board and lodging ought to come a little cheaper."

"Precisely. The maid will show you your sleeping-room—and, of course, the

entire house is at your service. I hope
you will find everything to your comfort. I am very anxious to please." He
laughed a little.

Elvira gave him a grateful, but at the
same time a rather patronizing, glance.
He felt at once that in carrying out his
little *ruse* he had placed himself deliberately upon a questionable footing with
the beautiful girl. He hoped, however,
to redeem himself by impressing her
with his knowledge of the pursuit which,
he accurately judged, had brought the
ladies to the city. Archibald had at one
time done a little painting himself. He
had dreamed dreams, as a young man,
which indolence and the stern business
atmosphere of the city had choked off
prematurely. As he looked down upon
the girl's sweet gray eyes a vision of
this youthful period came back to him.
Twenty-two and thirty-two have this in
common, that the latter age is not too

far away to quite despise the younger enthusiasm. Archibald at thirty-two still believed in himself, don't you know.

III.

SEVERAL days passed, during which the ladies settled themselves very readily in their new surroundings. They were very methodical, preferring to rise at an hour which, to Archibald, was something savoring of barbarism. He studied their habits, with a view to conforming to them as far as possible, but found that he could not bring himself to give up his nine-o'clock breakfasts, and so went to his club, leaving orders that the ladies should be accommodated at the earliest hour they might choose. He found that they had discovered Central Park, and came to make it a habit to stroll with them of a morning upon the Mall, and around the stagnant lakes. Central Park

was a novelty to him, except as seen
from horseback, or a four-in-hand, and
it really seemed very beautiful those summer mornings—he was really surprised,
don't you know! He wondered that
nice people did not use the Park more
—as they did Hyde Park in London.
As the days went on he filled his house
with flowers, turned the second floor
into an immense studio for Elvira, sat
about and watched her, criticised, en-
couraged her. He forgot Newport, forgot his polo. He had strangely ceased to
be bored. He was happy in New York
in midsummer! Dick Trellis told his
polo friends at Newport that Archibald
was probably undergoing private treat-
ment for softening of the brain, which
theory, in fact, they deemed sufficiently
complimentary.

As for his mother and sisters in Europe
—why, pray, should he inform them of
his little joke?

Elvira worked away at her easel when the light was best—during the after-noon. In the evening, after dinner, the ladies became socially inclined. It was then that they allowed Archibald to smoke in the " studio " and talk Art with Elvira. Indeed he found it very diffi-cult to talk anything else with the shy New England primrose.

About Art—with a big A—she was rapturous. There seemed to be in her soul a strange hunger for everything ornate and richly beautiful. Archibald devoted himself to studying her. He became strangely interested in East Village, Vt., where, he gathered, the Hon. Ephraim B. Price, her father, was a very distinguished Republican law-yer and politician. He drew Aunt Per-kins out concerning her Congregational church, her minister, her fear of the Catholics, her fondness for cats, her se-cret disbelief in Art. Once in a while

they read him a letter from the Hon.
Ephraim, in which he could see reflected
their own liking for *him*. He found that
he was spoken of as " Landlord Archibald." The Hon. Ephraim was a shrewd
old fellow, however, and his counsels and
advice were generally of the " trust-not-
too-much-to-appearances " order. One
evening Miss Perkins complained of a
headache, and Archibald found himself
alone for an hour with Elvira. She
sat beneath the rich brazen lamp, with
its pretty crimson shade, absorbing
some of the red glow in her lovely
face. They had been two weeks in the
city, and out of delicate feeling had
deposited two ten-dollar bills upon the
mantelpiece in the library, where Archibald would see them. He had roared
with laughter over them and intended
having them framed, but ultimately he
found a different use for their amusing
board-money.

He made some little allusion to the time they had been with him.

"Two very short weeks," said Elvira, "and you have been so very unusually kind, Mr. Archibald. You have done so much for us. We have noticed it. Is it usual for landlords to—to do so much, in the city?"

"It depends," he said, gravely. "Landlords do more for people who are congenial—you are congenial——"

"Oh!" A slight pause.

"You are more than congenial, *really*," said Archibald. "For you take an interest, Miss Price. I have secretly espied both you and your aunt dusting——"

Elvira bit her lip. "We *have* dusted," she admitted, reddening a little, "but it is merely out of force of habit."

"Really," said Archibald, "I rawther like you the better for it, don't you know!"

"I'm afraid," said Elvira, her face

lighting up with conscious pleasure, "that you have made up your mind as a landlord to like us, whatever we do. I'm afraid you would not like it at all if you knew everything that aunt has done."

" Tell me—I will keep it a profound secret, I assure you," he laughed.

" She has actually dared to invade your kitchen ! "

" Has she ? " said Archibald, dubiously ; " really ! "

" Yes, and she declares that your cook wastes enough every day to keep four families ! "

" Really ! " said Archibald ; " I'll have to look into it.";

" You won't save much out of what we pay," said Elvira, " and we don't want to stay if it doesn't pay you ; but——"

" Well ? "

" Mr. Archibald, we are poor." She looked down.

" I'm very sorry, I'm sure—I—" he

really did feel a compassion which found
its way into his voice, and made it trem-
ble a little.

"Aunt says you *can't* be making any
money. Now, we don't think it is right
to stay another day and be *burdens*, do
you see?"

A solemn pause.

"Isn't that what they are talking about
so much now in the novels?" he asked,
at length.

"What?"

"The terrible New England conscience?"

"Right is right and wrong is wrong,
Mr. Archibald, disguise it how we may,"
and Elvira compressed her pretty lips
firmly.

Archibald puffed on his cigar, lazily.

"I wasn't sure," he said, as if a doubt
had crept into his mind.

She glanced at him impatiently.

"Can't you *see* how wrong it would be

for us to stay here and enjoy all we have
in your beautiful house, knowing that we
were swindling you?" She stamped her
foot. "Mercy!" she added, half to herself, "what *can* you be made of?"

He hastened to a display of rugged conscience, which relieved her.

"Oh, of course, I see how wicked it
would be if you *did* swindle; but I'm
making money! Really—I haven't spent
the twenty dollars board-money yet. Oh,
pray rest assured—I shan't lose. I will
tell you when I run behind."

A great sense of relief seemed to come
over the girl.

"But it is all we can pay. I told father
I would not ask for more. Father said he
knew it would take more, but I said I
would give up Art first."

"Oh, I say!" he protested.

"And to-morrow I am going to begin
taking lessons, but I *will* not call on father for another cent. He shan't be able

to throw it in my face that it turned out as he said, and that I was wrong. When he and I dispute it always does turn out as he says—this time it *shan't*."

Archibald laughed a little. The poor fool, don't you know, was so captivated that every word, every action of the girl was music to him. The two weeks of observation had told on her dress. To-night she wore a white muslin, elaborated with pretty ribbons. She no longer seemed especially rustic to him. He noticed that she was doing her hair now in the prevailing style. "By Jove!" he said to himself, "I'll see that she comes out at the Patriarchs' next winter!"

This was his highest earthly happiness for a *débutante*.

"I am going to make money," she went on; "I'm going to paint vases, plates, odds and ends, pot-boilers, you know, and so father shan't know what it costs."

" Oh, by the way, if you do," he pretended, lazily blowing out a ring of
smoke, " I happen to know a fellow—an
old friend of mine—who gives very fair
prices for those sort of things. Now, I
am sure he will take any gimcrack you
may do."

Somehow the word gimcrack displeased
her.

" My Art work has always been thought
very pretty in East Village," she said.
" It would never *sell*, but it was thought
pretty. I used to long to help father—
and our family is so large, you know, four
little brothers and two sisters younger
than I am—and now, if I only *could* get
on, and help father! Oh, Mr. Archibald,
you don't know how *little* law there is to
go round in East Village!" She heaved
a deep sigh.

He tried to appear sympathetic.

" I know a fellow who gets a thousand
dollars for a portrait, and he has only

just commenced. You can't help but succeed, Miss Price, really ! "

She gave him a grateful glance.

" Oh, if I *could!* " she said, anxiously.
" I taught school one winter, but the pay
was so small. And I've tried—you will
laugh, Mr. Archibald, at my telling you
these things—but I've tried story writing.
I was *so* hopeful about it, and it took as
many as ten rejections before I became
convinced; and now, if my Art fails
me——"

She gave a little fluttering sigh.

" I think you have talent."

" Perhaps it is only enthusiasm——"

" That amounts to the same thing. It
will keep you up to your work. They
used to tell me I had talent, but I had no
enthusiasm, so I dropped it. I wish to
encourage you," he added ; " I hope you
will go on. It takes a lot of work, but
you have just the right temperament.
You *will* work. You *will* get on, and

when you become celebrated, Miss Price, you won't forget your old friends ? "

He realized that it was a rather bold step forward, and he trembled for her reply.

" I shall always recommend your house," she said, a little stiffly, making him feel more than ever her aristocratic superiority to landlords, " and I shall always remember your kindness. We went to at least six boarding-houses until we saw your sign — we saw the landladies. Really, Mr. Archibald, you have no idea how vulgar and unartistic *most* of the houses were. There was always a disagreeable odor, as if somebody was frying something. If I *do* succeed, as I wish, and make friends, and get to be known, and all, you may be certain that I shan't forget you. I may organize an Art class, and take the whole house myself ! "

He went no further. It was enough to him, as he sat opposite her in his evening dress, his rich opal, set with diamonds, flashing on his white shirt-front, his lawn tie, low shoes, white waistcoat—everything in the latest and most expensive style — it was enough for Mr. Jerome Archibald to sit there and smoke his delicate Havana, and reflect that he at least had her promise to do what she could to recommend his boarding-house !

The next day, at dinner, he again suggested, in an offhand way, that Miss Price should turn her attention to portrait-painting. Miss Perkins seriously objected at once.

"Your father would never give his consent," she said. "There was old Mr. Raymond, who lived on the Poor Farm, because he found portrait-painting didn't pay."

"Mr. Raymond painted dreadful, hideous caricatures," said Elvira. "He painted my mother's portrait, and father is always throwing him in my face. But

I don't know. I have no one to begin
on except aunt, and I have tried and
tried, and I can't get anything but the
expression of her spectacles."

Even Aunt Perkins laughed at this a
little.

" Begin on me," ventured Archibald.
" Call it the ' Portrait of an Ideal Landlord.' "

There was a little pause. The ladies
rose without replying, and Archibald followed them into the drawing-room, feeling indefinitely that he had been too forward. As he lit his cigar and sat near an
open window, feeling the cool southern
breeze, he reflected that it was not im-
probable that in East Village the only
landlord known to them was the keeper
of a common tavern. It amused him to
think of their primitive, quaint ignorance
of city ways. He pictured the small life
of East Village, Vt., the narrow social
horizon, the strange interest in politics,

the religious intolerance, the "strong" views on the temperance question which obtained there, and which leaked out from Miss Perkins as the days went on into August. The easy sense of accommodation to their new surroundings also amused him.

Archibald returned to the portrait. " I'd rawther like to have one for the dining-room," he said ; " I think it would interest some of my boarders when they come back next winter. I could give you no end of sittings, Miss Price——"

Elvira exhibited some hesitancy :

" Well, I might try," she said. " But I'm not at all good at hair——"

" Shave off my mustache if you like," said the infatuated Archibald, with a grimace.

The ladies changed the subject decorously. It was plain that Archibald's little advances toward an intimacy, to be derived from portrait-painting, were being

met in rather an unencouraging spirit,
don't you know! The next day he invited them, as an agreeable diversion, to
visit Coney Island; but Elvira made an
excuse that she had no time for " pleasur-
ing." They seemed, indeed, to have few
pleasures. The morning walk in Central
Park was given up; Miss Perkins spent
the greater part of the time when Elvira
was at the Art School in riding to and
fro, apparently, upon street-cars. One day
she came home very late to dinner, say-
ing that she had discovered the " Belt
Line." While waiting her return for dinner, Archibald had an agreeable *tête-à-
tête* with Elvira.

IV.

He was growing more and more in love
with this self-contained, charming, young
New Englander. It had come to a time
when he felt that he must speak. They

had been at No. 41 now these four weeks, aunt and niece, and yet they had managed to preserve their distance. He was no nearer than the day they arrived.

He reflected that the pleasant little daily comedy which had amused him so entirely would have to be given up the instant he made known to her his state of feeling. But at the same time he felt he could act out the equivocation no longer. He must, as a gentleman, make a clean breast of his deception. Archibald had seen a great deal of women, and he believed that he understood them pretty well. He believed he understood Miss Price well enough to reckon upon the flattery of her sudden fascination that first day, for him, as the cause of his deceit. He planned to boldly tell her this, one day, while they were waiting for Miss Perkins to revolve around the " Belt Line." But Elvira turned the conversation against his will. She seemed to have remarkable intuitions, this strange creature! Perhaps she had an intuition then. At any rate, she announced their determination to return to East Village the following Saturday.

" Father writes that his ague is no better — that I must come home," she said. " There are, besides, the preserves——"

Archibald expressed no surprise. " If you go," he said, " I think I'll take a run up there also. I have the greatest curiosity about East Village."

" There is nothing—it is dreadfully—I wouldn't have you visit East Village for all the world ! "

" Why ? "

" Because—" she replied, sedately.

Recognizing this as a sufficient reply, Archibald took a seat on the sofa near her. She was in one of her pretty, soft, white muslins, tied, this evening, with ribbons of the very latest shade of fashionable apple-green. He had noticed the steady growth

of fashion in the girl's appearance, but he
was not quite prepared for the dozen silver bangles, which jingled as she raised
her hand to her hair. She had a pretty
arm and hand, and were it not for the
bangles, which somehow altered the cur-
rent of his thought, he had nerved himself
up to the point of taking, or trying to-
take, her hand in his, and telling her in a
manly way his story. The bangles, however, don't you know, diverted him. He
could not be serious. He laughed. It
was as if he had happened upon a wood
nymph in seven-button kid gloves! She
misinterpreted his laughter, believing that
he intended to ridicule the pastoral delights of East Village.

" I'm not ashamed of Vermont," she
said, drawing away a little. " I can't
bear to have it laughed at. You would
laugh at East Village, Mr. Archibald—
you laugh at everything. You are not
sincere. You have too much of the city

in you — too much of its glitter and —"
She caught his eyes directed laughingly
upon her bangles, and blushed guiltily.

"Time works its changes, don't you
know," he said. "Even you, Miss Elvira, are a *little* affected."

"I hate myself for it," she said; "I *do*
find myself growing to like things I never
cared for before. I think of what I have
on from morning to night," she confessed,
guiltily, with an imploring glance at her
landlord.

"Can the dead dulness of midsummer
in the city have wrought so wondrous a
change?" he laughed. "How very gay,
really, you will be next winter."

"Seriously," said Elvira, "I look forward to a visit to East Village as a complete change and rest. When I think of
the white, dead walls of our meeting-
house, I am glad; when I think of the
lack of color in everybody up there, it
makes me glad; when I think of the plain-

ness of everything, the simpleness, the *truth* of everything, I'm glad to go back. But don't you—don't come up to Vermont, Mr. Archibald. Really, please, don't."

Again Archibald felt impelled to seize her white, pretty hand, and tell his story. He had never come to so intimate a point before. What chance had he ever to come so near again ? All that his mother and sisters could write would have no effect upon him now. All that his friends at the club would say, all that his Aunt Newbold would say—his Aunt Newbold was the formidable dragon of his family —nothing, he felt sure, would alter his mind. He had deliberated a month, he would deliberate no more. Besides, she was going away ; perhaps if he did *not* speak his opportunity would never again occur. He paled a little as he was about to open his lips.

Bother !

The chalk-faced maid entered with a card on a silver tray.

V.

MR. JEROME ARCHIBALD had very few hatreds ; people whom he disliked he carefully avoided.   Being fastidious to an extreme, he had few friends, but he likewise had no enemies.   He had, however, a certain cousin who lived in Boston, who had in some way early offended him, and for whom he continued to have a most inexplicable dislike.   Hunnewell Hollis was a Harvard man, who had been a great swell at college, and who was considered "clevah."   He was a year or two older than Archibald, and he usually presumed a little upon his age and upon his superior education.   It was Hunnewell Hollis's card which was brought up on the silver tray.

Archibald impatiently rose and went

down to the reception-room. There he found Hollis walking up and down the room, apparently in some excitement.

" Jerry, this won't do, old man !—heard ladies' voices up-stairs ! 'Twon't do ! Lucky I ran down with the yacht. Now I'm going to carry you off with me. By the way, Somers and Billy Nahant and Jack Chadwick are here, and I took the liberty to invite them here overnight—knew you were alone—knew you would be glad to put them up."

" By Jove, you do me great honor ! Unfortunately I haven't room for you—I've only just let the house—taken—by Jove ! I must take in the sign."

Archibald's face betrayed no sign of his justifiable prevarication.

" Well, then, as it is dinner-time I'll stay to dinner with you."

" Sorry, very sorry. But the ladies who have taken the house would think it very odd——"

" Well, how in the devil are *you* dining with them, Jerry ? "

" They asked me, in order to discuss the terms. A few details before signing the lease, don't you know ! "

" Well, it puts me in a rather awkward position ; I've left the fellows your address ; they'll be here shortly."

" Why don't you head 'em off? " suggested Archibald, coolly.

Mr. Hunnewell Hollis gave his cousin a glance of anger. " The whole thing is rather fishy," he said, suspiciously. " I trust, Jerry, for the honor of the family——"

Archibald never quite detested his cousin so much before.

" There are a great many adventuresses about ; they are on the lookout for rich young men like you, Jerry," and Hunnewell Hollis, giving his cousin a rather gravely serious nod, took up his hat and cane and departed.

Archibald went directly upstairs. He
heard a rustle of a dress against the furniture. Had Elvira been listening? He
hoped not.

VI.

ADVENTURESS! How that odious word
rang in his ears as he entered the room
where the sweet primrose face was still
in its corner of the sofa. He swore he
would never write to, nor speak to, Hunnewell Hollis again. He had done with
him forever. Yet, had he heard the rustle
of her dress? It gave him a slightly disagreeable sensation to think that it were
possible. Elvira Price apparently had
not moved from her seat. She was in the
same pretty attitude in which he had left
her, leaning back, easily, against the corner of the sofa, her hands crossed in her
lap. As he entered it seemed to him that
she was studying his face.

" I was so anxious about aunt," she

said. "I went out to the stairs thinking I heard her come in. Do you know, it isn't the Belt Line only; she goes to a mission—a boy's mission. She has taken the greatest interest in it; all the teachers have gone away for the summer. It is in an out-of-the-way part of the city, and it worries me."

Archibald hesitated a moment, then he said:

"Did you hear the row with my cousin? He was very impertinent; but all Bostonians are impertinent."

The name Bostonian seemed to give her a slight sensation.

"You have been in Boston?" he asked.

"N—yes, and I, too, found Bostonians impertinent." She gave him an appealing glance; then she added, after a pause, "I find New York quite different."

Miss Perkins came in shortly after, much fatigued, and Archibald after dinner went over to the club, where he fell in with Hunnewell Hollis again, in spite of the fact that he did his best to avoid him.   Hunnewell had found his yachting friends, and they had had a very good dinner.   They were all very talkative— Somers, Billy Nahant, and Jack Chadwick.   They were in flannel suits and yachting caps, and each was bronzed and sunburned to a fine copper hue.

"What is the name of the people who have taken your house?" asked Hunnewell, bluntly, after he had introduced Archibald to his friends.

"Miss Perkins and her niece, Miss Elvira Price," replied Archibald, coldly.

Instantly Billy Nahant pricked up his ears.   "Why," he said, "isn't she an actress?   Didn't she play in Boston last winter?"

"Who?" asked Archibald.

"Why, Elvira Price.   She made quite a hit, I believe—her *début* too—at the Boston Theatre.   She played to crowded

houses exactly two weeks ; at the end
of that time, to everyone's surprise, she
went home to Vermont, whence she came,
and she calmly gave up the stage forever ! "

Archibald's face was a study.

" Did you know you were letting your
mother's house to actresses ? " asked Hollis, with a sneer.

" Miss Price is probably a different person from the one to whom Mr. Nahant
has reference," said Archibald, coldly.

" I remember the girl," said Jack Chadwick. " She was very young and beautiful, and fitted her part admirably. She
made an excellent *ingénue*. She held
herself well—not at all gushing, don't you
know—but poetic, *spirituelle*. She played
in ' A Scrap of Paper '—some picked-up
company with her. She carried the play
very well. I have often wondered what
became of her."

" So this is the creature who has rented

your house, and whom you dined with to-
night," sneered Hollis ; " an *ingénue*,
indeed ! "

" Miss Price is a lady—not a 'creature,' " said Archibald, haughtily. " As
far as I have seen, she can only honor
our house by remaining under its roof."
And Archibald bowed stiffly, and took
his leave in the midst of an embarrassed
silence.

VII.

. HE preferred not to see Elvira again
before she took her departure for Vermont the next day. Her aunt remained
in the city to look after her " mission
work." Archibald presented her, as the
gift of a rich, unknown friend, fifty dollars
—their board money—to send some of
her boys into the country. After Elvira's
departure he became very despondent.
Elvira's image was broken to him, and
while she had not become in his mind

quite an adventuress, yet she had concealed her former life from him.   She had
deceived him.

But as the days went by and he missed
her, he found that he must speak to Miss
Perkins about Elvira's acting, or go
through a serious case of nervous pros-
tration.   He said very bluntly to her, one
day, at dinner :

" So I hear your niece is a great actress."

Miss Perkins gave him a quick, sharp
glance.

" She *has* acted," she replied.   " But
Elvira Price had too much conscience to
act *long*."

He gave a sigh of relief.

" She acted in Boston, because she
was bound to try it.   She wanted to try
everything—everything that would keep
her father out of the poor-house and edu-
cate the family.   But acting, Mr. Archibald, is a dreadful business !   As soon as

Elvira saw into it a little she quit. The air wasn't pure enough, somehow, for her. Elvira, she needs awful pure air ! "

Again Archibald felt a certain glow of satisfaction steal over him.

" Do you know," he said, after a suitable pause, " I am more than half-inclined to make her angry by running up to East Village."

Miss Perkins gave a little quinzied laugh of satisfaction. She was beginning to like Archibald very much.

" It would startle Elvira ; but she'd be pleased," ventured the thin old maid. " She'd be pleased—in spite of everything ! "

A few days later Archibald, after half a day's journey, found himself in Vermont. As the train drew near East Village the mountains grew higher and the scenery wilder. He could see the great August moon roll itself above the high crest of the mountains to the west. Though

Archibald was far from superstitious, he was pained to observe that he saw the moon over his left shoulder.

It was late when he stumbled from the steps of the car upon the wooden platform of the station at East Village. It was dark, also, and to him, extraordinarily cold. He groped his way, shivering, past a blinding reflector, where half a dozen men in cow-hide boots were examing a list of invoices, to what he could dimly outline as the village stage. No one spoke to him, and he found that no one seemed to care whether he, the sole passenger, was carried. He had visions of an unpleasant nature, of being deposited inside the coach in a shed or stable to await the morning. He felt the stage pitch and toss for twenty minutes like a bark upon an angry sea. When all was still again he found that the driver had drawn up before a white-pillared old-fashioned house, which stood a little back

from the street. At the side of the gate
a small wooden building bore the sign,
which was illuminated by the stage lamp,

Ephraim B. Price, Attorney at Law.

" Oh," said Archibald, " this is Elvira's
house, and the driver is delivering my
box of flowers."

He leaned forward, hoping to catch
sight of the fair young girl when the front-
door opened to take in the box. But he
was disappointed. The impatient driver
had merely left it on the steps of the
high, white - pillared portico, after giving
the door-bell a vigorous pull.

Then followed a further few minutes of
pitching and tossing, and the stage drew
up before the tavern-door. A row of a
dozen men, whose hats were drawn down
over their eyes, and whose feet fell instan-
taneously from the rail to the floor as the
coach drew up, came forward, and one of
them betrayed a desire to grasp Archi-

bald's in his own horny hand. " Guess
ye'll stop overnight ? Th'ain't no other
place. 'Sprised to see a stranger to-night,
tew. Will you go in an' sign—will you,
sir ? "

" So this uncouth ruffian," thought
Archibald, " is Elvira's ideal landlord !
No wonder she distrusts me ! "

" We're local temp'rance," said the
landlord. " An' no licker's being seen to
East Village for nigh six years. Not a
drop, sir, an' it's bustin' my ho-tel higher'n a kite. Yes; it is ! "

Archibald expressed commiseration.

" As I tell'd Squar' Price, ' yeou high-
toned, 'ristocratic temp'rance folk'll hurt
East Village when ye close the hotel ! '
Why, when a gent comes up here fr' the
city, he wants to be able to call fer a
glass o' gin or a glass o' whiskey 's often
's he likes."

Archibald thought he detected the faint
smell of liquor upon the landlord's breath

as he talked, and it occurred to him that his obtrusively free-and-easy-manner was the result of a secret violation of the prohibitory local license law. " Bein' fr' the city, as you be," said the landlord, lowering his voice to a whisper, and placing his heavy hand on Archibald's shoulder familiarly, " I calc'late you're cold an' ready for a tidy drink. I calc'late I'm talkin' to a gent as is used 'ter lickerin' up, even ef 'tis agin the law ? " To humor him, Archibald admitted that he had no stringent prohibitory sentiments.

" Well then, good ! Jest you foller me ! "

Archibald followed the landlord out into the hotel yard, where the latter pulled up the flaps of a cellar-door. Hearing the creaking sound, and taking it for an admonitory signal, the row of men on the hotel piazza, who had resumed their seats, again dropped their feet on the floor, rose, and came out into the yard in Indian file, in perfect silence. Archibald followed his landlord down into the darkness of the cellar, where, beneath the dim light of a solitary candle he perceived a cask with a wooden spigot, and near it half a dozen tin cups. The men filed down the steps behind him. " You've heerd o' apple jack ? " asked the landlord, in a whisper.

Archibald nodded.

" Drink that, then ! " and the landlord handed him a cupful of the beverage. It was enough to intoxicate him. He drank but a very little ; as he saw the other men were waiting, he passed the cup on to them.

" Welcome to East Village, stranger," said one of the men, drinking. " Be you up 'ere a-sellin' marchandize ? "

" Oh, no ! "

" Be you come to see the Squar' ? "

" Well—perhaps—yes."

" Wa'l, this is a dead give away ! " and the men laughed noisily, as rustics will.

" Don't mention this 'ere cider to Squar' Price ! "

The next morning was delicious, the air clear and smelling of the mountains. The mist hung above the distant river, and a line of hills showed their green wooded outline above it. As Archibald breathed the sweet country air, he stepped more briskly, felt less of his city malaria, drew into his lungs a long breath of the fresh, invigorating summer wind, which seemed to come to him across the high upland, from such a vast distance.

He came to the old colonial gate and entered. The Hon. Ephraim B. Price was just at the moment sauntering down the gravel path from his house to his law office. As he saw Archibald enter, he came forward somewhat more rapidly. He was a man of large frame, gaunt rather than spare, of prominent cheekbones, of lengthy chin-beard. His eyes

were very keen, and his entire expression
was one of patient alertness—as if there
was very little to be alert over, but a deep
necessity of keeping up a reputation.
Archibald learned afterward how indefatigable a partisan, and how strenuous
a believer in the Republican party the
Hon. Ephraim was.

" Sir," he said, after greeting Archibald, and looking with a grin of pity upon
his engraved card—a grin directed chiefly
to the " Mr." before Archibald's name—
" you are Elvira's landlord down to New
York—tell me, how is your city and State
going, do you think ? "

Archibald felt taken aback. Politics
were something of which he knew nothing.   He was but barely aware that it was
a presidential year.   In the city he kept
severely out of politics, as hardly the em-
ployment of gentlemen.

" I—I—think it will go Democratic."

A more violent frown than before.   " If

I thought so, sir ; if I imagined so ; if for one instant I believed that what we fought for during the war—Eh, Elvira ? Here is Mr. Archibald ! "

Then the Hon. Ephraim turned abruptly and entered his office, where, it may be added, he sat for the next hour, his feet on the cold stove before him, meditating where his next fee was to come from, and breaking out with an occasional invective against the wicked democracy.

Before the old gentleman was a square window which looked out over the town. All day long he sat before this, as upon a watch-tower—a censor of village morals and deportment.

"Father is so interested in the election," apologized Elvira. "But how strange to see you here ; and I told you not to ! "

She held a small gray kitten in her arms, which she stroked slowly. She was still in his favorite white muslin, and she had a gentle, sweet flush of pleasure in her face.

" I came, Miss Price—because—don't you know—I—aw—missed you," and he smiled.

" You are very good. How is Aunt Perkins ? Did she bring her mission boys to your house ? She has written that a friend of yours has given fifty dollars for the boys. Do tell me about it. Is she well ? Have any more boarders come ? "

She plied him with questions as they strolled toward the white-pillared portico. The house was old and shabby, but he did not notice it. The place was run down and impoverished, but it seemed very beautiful to him, for he noticed that she wore one of his roses in her lustrous hair.

Entering the hallway he met some of the younger brothers and sisters, and felt a sudden strange affection spring up in his heart for them. Elvira took him through into a gloomy parlor, lined with plain hair-cloth furniture. On the walls were several portraits. "This was my mother," said the girl, affectionately, pointing to what Archibald felt to be a hideous daub, a red-faced woman in black, against a green background. It was the portrait by Mr. Raymond, whose abode was now the poor-house. "She died only two years ago——"

"I fancy if she had lived," said Archibald, "you would not have tried—the stage?"

She looked at him calmly a moment.

"That Boston man has told you?"

"Yes, I learned the fact from his friends."

"I shall never—again." There was a despairing pathos in her voice.

"Elvira," he said, slowly, "as I see it —I think it was very noble of you to try."

Then, unaccountably to him, she burst into tears.

" It is what I love—what I long for—
to be an actress—a great actress," she
sobbed. " But I can't—I can't! I can't
exist with those creatures—those horrible
men who hang about you! No one knows
what I endured! No one knows what,
too, I gave up when I left the stage and
came home ; but I *had* to."

He leaned forward in sympathy.

" You may say what you will, but there
is no Art like acting, and nothing so fine
as applause. Oh, that I could bring myself to do it—to be strong enough to do it
—to save our fortunes—to help father.
You little know how I have suffered, Mr.
Archibald."

" By Jove—I—I quite like you for it ! "

He was on his feet at her side. Impulsively he bent down and whispered close
to her ear. " Let me be your audience
the rest of my life ! Act for *me*—let me
applaud everything — anything you do,
my darling ! always ! always ! "

She put him away.

"I don't feel 1 have acted just right *with* you," she said. "I should have told you that I was—or might be again—an actress." She spoke coldly. "I don't believe you want them in your boarding-house. They are not always desirable, I believe!" Elvira's eyes were fastened on the floor.

Archibald paced to and fro in the parlor. "Confound her odd New England conscience!" he muttered to himself. Seizing her hands, he cried, passionately, "I, too, must confess. Elvira, I loved you that first day you came. *I loved you !* Therefore I let you think—it *was* a boarding house."

"And it isn't—it's your own private— Oh, Mr. Archibald!"

She sat and looked at him with a horrified stare. The full truth of his imposition began to steal upon her gradually. Then her face fell and she averted it, as

she felt that a fatal untruth had come between them. She rose quietly and left
him standing near her. She went up-
stairs to her room and threw herself upon
her bed in an agony of tears.

Through it all Archibald had merely
smiled !

VIII.

BUT when she left him he felt rather
weak for a moment, as if his city malaria
had returned upon him with a double
force. As Elvira showed no signs of re-
turning, he amused himself by turning
over the leaves of the family photograph
album. Face by face revealed the stern,
set, arid, Puritan features, the hard, determined chins, and the "firmness," which,
in the person of the Hon. Ephraim, he
felt still dominated and controlled the
public affairs of East Village. He threw
down the album with a feeling of impo-
tent rage against the survival of this co-

lonial "narrowness," as he liked to call
it. He walked out of the house and wan-
dered, much crestfallen and full of malaria, along the village street toward the
hotel. A great many farm wagons were
tied along the sidewalk, and there were
numbers of fresh-cheeked country girls
walking in threes and fours, and sweeping
the sidewalk as they went. Upon a slight
elevation stood a white wooden meeting-
house, with a white steeple, and it gave
him a chill even on that warm morning
to look at it—it *looked* so cold. Small
groups of hard-featured farmers in fur
caps stood on the corners of the streets
discussing, presumably, the crops. He
wondered if the fur caps were needed in
that arid, bleak region to keep warm the
natives' sense of Right and Wrong? He
made his way out, beneath some beautiful
elms, into a small, old-fashioned burying-
ground, where he discovered that "erring
sinners" apparently comprised the only

element of those who were requested to
"*Pause and Read.*" Feeling himself to
be now, for some reason, a distinctly im-
moral person, he read some of the quaint
epitaphs, to which he was invited, in a
spirit of humility, which presently changed
to amusement. In death as in life, the
hard, stern old village characters pre-
served on their headstones a fund of grim
humor for the "sinner," which in Archibald's instance made him smile. "Oh,"
he sighed to himself, "I long to take her
away from all this sort of thing—forever!"

He took a long walk in the afternoon,
and returned to the hotel to find a coldly
worded note from Elvira inviting him
around to tea. He removed the stains of
his walk, and dressed himself with his
usual care. He found Elvira waiting for
him beneath the high white pillars, in an
unbecoming, and as it seemed to him, for-
bidding dress of black. Her face seemed

unusually stern and relentless. There
were traces of tears in her red eyelids,
but the tears were dried away now, and
her eyes were very bright and hard.

" Don't say anything *now*. Father feels
very deeply about it. We have had a
long talk. When he heard of the—of the
unfortunate house affair—he was *so* angry
I could hardly pacify him."

Archibald's heart sank within him. He
fairly shivered.

" He said that he did not want me to
lower my standard," continued Elvira, in
her clear, musical, passionless voice.
" And I told him that he need have no
fears. I wanted to see you first, and tell
you. Let us not have any *feeling* about it."

" Any *feeling* !" exclaimed Archibald.
" Why—how can we help it ! "

" Let us act as if we had never understood one another. I will go back to the
city with you, and Aunt Perkins and I will
find some other place at once."

" Go back with me—and expect me to show no feeling! Elvira, this is preposterous! "

" Then I will go back alone." She compressed her lips, just as he had observed her father do.

" I beg pardon. Elvira, do you mean—can you mean that I can never—I can never hope! "

She nodded her pretty flower-like head gravely. "Come in to tea, won't you ? " she said, coolly. " I want father to hear you talk about Art."

He turned on his heel. At last he, too, was angry.

" Thanks, awfully," he said. " But if I go back to the hotel now, I shall just have time to pack my valise and catch the evening train."

He walked rapidly away, leaving her standing upon the white-pillared portico, looking with pure, sweet, upturned face, like a saint who has for all time renounced

the world, the flesh, and the devil. Had
he looked back, Mr. Jerome Archibald's
tender heart would have been touched by
her attitude ; he would have returned,
and, against her will, clasped her in his
arms and covered her pale lips with warm
kisses. It might have melted her high
" standard " a little. But he let a night
intervene without seeing her, and the entering wedge of her high sense of duty did
its work before morning. He determined
to remain another day and make a further
trial. When he called the next day she
was obdurate. " Love cannot be built
upon deceit and untruth," she said, sen-
tentiously. " I was not frank, you were
not. It is better that we should part. I
could never hold up my head—I could
never face the world. I know what they
would call me. They would call me an
adventuress! and they would hate me for
being successful. Yes — your mother,
your sisters—everyone."

" But you were perfectly innocent about it, Elvira."

There was a little pause.

" I, too, was innocent. I meant no more than to have you near me, where I could learn to know you—love you—and now, really, it seems as if you had built up a mountain of ice between us, don't you know."

She merely shook her head.

When Archibald returned to the city his malaria compelled him to go away again almost immediately to Newport. There, a few weeks later, his agent wrote him that he had succeeded in renting the house " at an exorbitant figure to a very rich tenant without children."—thus fulfilling his mother's conditions to the letter. He went back to the city, recovered in health, to pack up a few personal effects, and found to his surprise that Miss Perkins and her niece were, at the moment he arrived, in the house. They had taken board on Ninth Street, and had gone up to take a last look of the charming interior where, Elvira guiltily acknowledged, life had been "so wrongly pleasant." He found Elvira holding a fan in her hand and seated pensively in an old Venetian chair in what was formerly her studio. As he entered the room she rose, blushing a most vivid red, and as rapidly turning pale again.

"Mr. Archibald!" she exclaimed. "I did not know you were in the city!"

"I have been here only an hour," he said, stiffly.

"It is time for us to go;" and she turned to the door.

"Elvira!" His face looked sick and ghastly.

"Well?" She drew herself up very coldly.

"Are you made of stone?"

"Mr. Archibald, what can you mean?"

"My child, you are capable of grinding

one who loves you into powder—like—er
—a millstone ! "

" Aunt Perkins ! " she called out, " let
us go ! "

" No," he cried, " I will not let you go.
You shall hear me !   I love you !   Do you
hear ?   And you shall not leave this house
until you say you will be my wife !   I
know you care for me—everything tells
me so—but you will wear your own and
my heart out with your hard, cruel conscience !   What brought you here ?   *You
loved me !*   Why have you been sitting in
this room ?   You love me, Elvira—I know
it—I feel it ! "

Gently he drew her to him and kissed
her.   She laid her head on his shoulder
and breathed a little contented sigh.   " *I
don't think this—is right !* " she said.

MRS. MANSTEY'S VIEW

By Edith Wharton

THE view from Mrs. Manstey's window was not a striking one, but to her at least it was full of interest and beauty. Mrs. Manstey occupied the back room on the third floor of a New York boarding-house, in a street where the ash-barrels lingered late on the sidewalk and the gaps in the pavement would have staggered a Quintus Curtius. She was the widow of a clerk in a large wholesale house, and his death had left her alone, for her only daughter had married in California, and could not afford the long journey to New York to see her mother. Mrs. Manstey, perhaps, might have joined her daughter in the West, but they had now been so many years apart that they had ceased to feel any need of each other's society, and their intercourse had long been limited to the exchange of a few perfunctory letters, written with indifference by the daughter, and with difficulty by Mrs. Manstey, whose right hand was growing stiff with gout. Even had she felt a stronger desire for her daughter's companionship, Mrs. Manstey's increasing infirmity, which caused her to dread the three flights of stairs between her room and the street, would have given her pause on the eve of undertaking so long a journey ; and without, perhaps, formulating these reasons she had long since accepted as a matter of course her solitary life in New York.

She was, indeed, not quite lonely, for a few friends still toiled up now and then to her room ; but their visits grew rare as the years went by. Mrs. Manstey had never

been a sociable woman, and during her
husband's lifetime his companionship had
been all-sufficient to her. For many years
she had cherished a desire to live in the
country, to have a hen-house and a gar-
den ; but this longing had faded with age,
leaving only in the breast of the uncom-
municative old woman a vague tenderness
for plants and animals. It was, perhaps,
this tenderness which made her cling so
fervently to the view from her window, a
view in which the most optimistic eye
would at first have failed to discover
anything admirable.

Mrs. Manstey, from her coign of van-
tage (a slightly projecting bow-window
where she nursed an ivy and a succession
of unwholesome-looking bulbs), looked
out first upon the yard of her own dwelling, of which, however, she could get but
a restricted glimpse.   Still, her gaze took
in the topmost boughs of the ailanthus below her window, and she knew how early

each year the clump of dicentra strung its bending stalk with hearts of pink.

But of greater interest were the yards beyond. Being for the most part attached to boarding-houses they were in a state of chronic untidiness and fluttering, on certain days of the week, with miscellaneous garments and frayed table-cloths. In spite of this Mrs. Manstey found much to admire in the long vista which she commanded. Some of the yards were, indeed, but stony wastes, with grass in the cracks of the pavement and no shade in spring save that afforded by the intermittent leafage of the clothes-lines. These yards Mrs. Manstey disapproved of, but the others, the green ones, she loved. She had grown used to their disorder ; the broken barrels, the empty bottles and paths unswept no longer annoyed her ; hers was the happy faculty of dwelling on the pleasanter side of the prospect before her.

In the very next enclosure did not a
magnolia open its hard white flowers
against the watery blue of April? And
was there not, a little way down the line,
a fence foamed over every May by lilac
waves of wistaria? Farther still, a
horse-chestnut lifted its candela-
bra of buff and pink blossoms
above broad fans of foliage;
while in the opposite yard
June was sweet with the
breath of a neglected sy-
ringa, which persisted in
growing in spite of the
countless obstacles op-
posed to its welfare.

But if nature occupied
the front rank in Mrs.
Manstey's v i e w , there
was much of a more per-
sonal character to inter-
est her in the aspect of
the houses and their in-

mates. She deeply disapproved of the
mustard-colored curtains which had late-
ly been hung in the doctor's window opposite ; but she glowed with pleasure
when the house farther down had its old
bricks washed with a coat of paint. The
occupants of the houses did not often
show themselves at the back windows,
but the servants were always in sight.
Noisy slatterns, Mrs. Manstey pro-
nounced the greater number ; she knew
their ways and hated them. But to the
quiet cook in the newly painted house,
whose mistress bullied her, and who
secretly fed the stray cats at nightfall,
Mrs. Manstey's warmest sympathies were
given. On one occasion her feelings
were racked by the neglect of a house-
maid, who for two days forgot to feed
the parrot committed to her care. On
the third day, Mrs. Manstey, in spite of
her gouty hand, had just penned a letter, beginning : " Madam, it is now

three days since your parrot has been
fed," when the forgetful maid appeared
at the window with a cup of seed in her
hand.

But in Mrs. Manstey's more medita-
tive moods it was the narrowing perspective of far-off yards which pleased
her best. She loved, at twilight, when
the distant brown-stone spire seemed
melting in the fluid yellow of the west,
to lose herself in vague memories of a
trip to Europe, made years ago, and now
reduced in her mind's eye to a pale
phantasmagoria of indistinct steeples
and dreamy skies. Perhaps at heart
Mrs. Manstey was an artist ; at all events
she was sensible of many changes of
color unnoticed by the average eye, and
dear to her as the green of early spring
was the black lattice of branches against
a cold sulphur sky at the close of a
snowy day. She enjoyed, also, the sunny
thaws of March, when patches of earth

showed through the snow, like ink-spots spreading on a sheet of white blotting-paper; and, better still, the haze of boughs, leafless but swollen, which replaced the clear-cut tracery of winter. She even watched with a certain interest the trail of smoke from a far-off factory chimney, and missed a detail in the landscape when the factory was closed and the smoke disappeared.

Mrs. Manstey, in the long hours which she spent at her window, was not idle. She read a little, and knitted numberless stockings; but the view surrounded and shaped her life as the sea does a lonely island. When her rare callers came it was difficult for her to detach herself from the contemplation of the opposite window-washing, or the scrutiny of certain green points in a neighboring flower-bed which might, or might not, turn into hyacinths, while she feigned an interest in her visitor's anecdotes about

some unknown grandchild. Mrs. Manstey's real friends were the denizens of
the yards, the hyacinths, the magnolia,
the green parrot, the maid who fed the
cats, the doctor who studied late behind
his mustard-colored curtains ; and the
confidant of her tenderer musings was
the church-spire floating in the sunset.

One April day, as she sat in her usual
place, with knitting cast aside and eyes
fixed on the blue sky mottled with round
clouds, a knock at the door announced
the entrance of her landlady.   Mrs. Manstey did not care for her landlady, but
she submitted to her visits with ladylike
resignation.   To-day, however, it seemed
harder than usual to turn from the blue
sky and the blossoming magnolia to Mrs.
Sampson's unsuggestive face, and Mrs.
Manstey was conscious of a distinct effort as she did so.

" 'The magnolia is out earlier than usual
this year, Mrs. Sampson," she remarked,

yielding to a rare impulse, for she seldom alluded to the absorbing interest of her life. In the first place it was a topic not likely to appeal to her visitors and, besides, she lacked the power of expression and could not have given utterance to her feelings had she wished to.

" The what, Mrs. Manstey ? " inquired the landlady, glancing about the room as if to find there the explanation of Mrs. Manstey's statement.

" The magnolia in the next yard—in Mrs. Black's yard," Mrs. Manstey repeated.

" Is it, indeed ? I didn't know there was a magnolia there," said Mrs. Sampson, carelessly. Mrs. Manstey looked at her ; she did not know that there was a magnolia in the next yard !

" By the way," Mrs. Sampson continued, " speaking of Mrs. Black reminds me that the work on the extension is to begin next week.

"The what?" it was Mrs. Manstey's turn to ask.

"The extension," said Mrs. Sampson, nodding her head in the direction of the ignored magnolia. "You knew, of course, that Mrs. Black was going to build an extension to her house? Yes, ma'am, I hear it is to run right back to the end of the yard. How she can afford to build an extension in these hard times I don't see; but she always was crazy about building. She used to keep a boarding-house in Seventeeth Street, and she near-ly ruined herself then by sticking out bow-windows and what not; I should have thought that would have cured her of build-ing, but I guess it's a disease, like drink. Anyhow, the work is to begin on Monday."

Mrs. Manstey had grown pale. She always spoke slowly, so the landlady did not heed the long pause which followed. At last Mrs. Manstey said: "Do you know how high the extension will be?"

" That's the most absurd part of it. The extension is to be built right up to the roof of the main building : now, did you ever ? "

Mrs. Manstey paused again. " Won't it be a great annoyance to you, Mrs. Sampson ? " she asked.

" I should say it would. But there's no help for it ; if people have got a mind to build extensions there's no law to prevent 'em, that I'm aware of." Mrs. Manstey, knowing this, was silent. " There is no help for it," Mrs. Sampson repeated, but if I *am* a church member, I wouldn't be so sorry if it ruined Eliza Black. Well, good-day, Mrs Manstey ; I'm glad to find you so comfortable."

So comfortable—so comfortable ! Left to herself the old woman turned once more to the window. How lovely the view was that day ! The blue sky with its round clouds shed a brightness over everything ; the ailanthus had put on a tinge of yellow-green, the hyacinths were budding, the magnolia flowers looked more than ever like rosettes carved in alabaster. Soon the wistaria would bloom, then the horse-chestnut; but not for her. Between her eyes and them a barrier of brick and mortar would swiftly rise; presently even the spire would disappear, and all her radiant world be blotted out. Mrs. Manstey sent away untouched the dinner-tray brought to her that evening. She lingered in the window until the windy sunset died in bat-colored dusk; then, going to bed, she lay sleepless all night.

Early the next day she was up and at the window. It was raining, but even through the slanting gray gauze the scene had its charm—and then the rain was so good for the trees. She had noticed the day before that the ailanthus was growing dusty.

"Of course I might move," said Mrs.

Manstey aloud, and turning from the window she looked about her room. She might move, of course; so might she be flayed alive; but she was not likely to survive either operation. The room, though far less important to her happiness than the view, was as much a part of her existence. She had lived in it seventeen years. She knew every stain on the wallpaper, every rent in the carpet; the light fell in a certain way on her engravings, her books had grown shabby on their shelves, her bulbs and ivy were used to their window and knew which way to lean to the sun. "We are all too old to move," she said.

That afternoon it cleared. Wet and radiant the blue reappeared through torn rags of cloud; the ailanthus sparkled; the earth in the flower-borders looked rich and warm. It was Thursday, and on Monday the building of the extension was to begin.

On Sunday afternoon a card was

brought to Mrs. Black, as she was engaged in gathering up the fragments of
the boarders' dinner in the basement.
The card, black-edged, bore Mrs. Manstey's name.

"One of Mrs. Sampson's boarders;
wants to move, I suppose. Well, I can
give her a room next year in the extension. Dinah," said Mrs. Black, "tell the
lady I'll be upstairs in a minute."

Mrs. Black found Mrs. Manstey standing in the long parlor garnished with
statuettes and antimacassars; in that
house she could not sit down.

Stooping hurriedly to open the register,
which let out a cloud of dust, Mrs. Black
advanced to her visitor.

"I'm happy to meet you, Mrs. Manstey; take a seat, please," the landlady
remarked in her prosperous voice, the
voice of a woman who can afford to build
extensions. There was no help for it;
Mrs. Manstey sat down.

" Is there anything I can do for you, ma'am ? " Mrs. Black continued. " My house is full at present, but I am going to build an extension, and——"

" It is about the extension that I wish to speak," said Mrs. Manstey, suddenly. " I am a poor woman, Mrs. Black, and I have never been a happy one. I shall have to talk about myself first to — to make you understand."

Mrs. Black, astonished but imperturbable, bowed at this parenthesis.

" I never had what I wanted," Mrs. Manstey continued. " It was always one disappointment after another. For years I wanted to live in the country. I dreamed and dreamed about it ; but we never could manage it. There was no sunny window in our house, and so all my plants died. My daughter married years ago and went away—besides, she never cared for the same things. Then my husband died and I was left alone.

That was seventeen years ago. I went
to live at Mrs. Sampson's, and I have
been there ever since. I have grown a
little infirm, as you see, and I don't get
out often ; only on fine days, if I am feeling very well. So you can understand
my sitting a great deal in my window—
the back window on the third floor——"

" Well, Mrs. Manstey," said Mrs.
Black, liberally, " I could give you a
back room, I dare say ; one of the new
rooms in the ex——"

" But I don't want to move ; I can't
move," said Mrs. Manstey, almost with
a scream. " And I came to tell you that
if you build that extension I shall have no
view from my window—no view ! Do you
understand ? "

Mrs. Black thought herself face to face
with a lunatic, and she had always heard
that lunatics must be humored."

" Dear me, dear me," she remarked,
pushing her chair back a little way, " that

is too bad, isn't it? Why, I never thought of that. To be sure, the extension *will* interfere with your view, Mrs. Manstey."

" You do understand ? " Mrs. Manstey gasped.

" Of course I do. And I'm real sorry about it, too. But there, don't you worry, Mrs. Manstey. I guess we can fix that all right."

Mrs. Manstey rose from her seat, and Mrs. Black slipped toward the door.

" What do you mean by fixing it ? Do you mean that I can induce you to change your mind about the extension ? Oh, Mrs. Black, listen to me. I have two thousand dollars in the bank and I could manage, I know I could manage, to give you a thousand if——" Mrs. Manstey paused ; the tears were rolling down her cheeks.

" There, there, Mrs. Manstey, don't you worry," repeated Mrs. Black, soothingly. " I am sure we can settle it. I

am sorry that I can't stay and talk about
it any longer, but this is such a busy
time of day, with supper to get——"

Her hand was on the door-knob, but
with sudden vigor Mrs. Manstey seized
her wrist

" You are not giving me a definite answer.   Do you mean to say that you accept my proposition ? "

" Why, I'll think it over, Mrs. Man·
stey, certainly I will.   I wouldn't annoy
you for the world——"

" But the work is to begin to-morrow, I
am told," Mrs. Manstey persisted.

Mrs. Black hesitated.   " It shan't begin, I promise you that ; I'll send word
to the builder this very night."   Mrs.
Manstey tightened her hold.

" You are not deceiving me, are you ? "
she said.

" No—no,"   stammered Mrs. Black.
" How can you think such a thing of me,
Mrs. Manstey ? "

Slowly Mrs. Manstey's clutch relaxed, and she passed through the open door. "One thousand dollars," she repeated, pausing in the hall; then she let herself out of the house and hobbled down the steps, supporting herself on the cast-iron railing.

"My goodness," exclaimed Mrs. Black, shutting and bolting the hall-door, "I never knew the old woman was crazy! And she looks so quiet and ladylike, too."

Mrs. Manstey slept well that night, but early the next morning she was awakened by a sound of hammering. She got to her window with what haste she might and, looking out, saw that Mrs. Black's yard was full of workmen. Some were carrying loads of brick from the kitchen to the yard, others beginning to demolish the old-fashioned wooden balcony which adorned each story of Mrs. Black's house. Mrs. Manstey saw that she had been deceived. At first she thought of confiding her trouble to Mrs. Sampson, but a settled discouragement soon took possession of her and she went back to bed, not caring to see what was going on.

Toward afternoon, however, feeling that she must know the worst, she rose and dressed herself. It was a laborious task, for her hands were stiffer than usual, and the hooks and buttons seemed to evade her.

When she seated herself in the window, she saw that the workmen had removed the upper part of the balcony, and that the bricks had multiplied since morning. One of the men, a coarse fellow with a bloated face, picked a magnolia blossom and, after smelling it, threw it to the ground; the next man, carrying a load of bricks, trod on the flower in passing.

"Look out, Jim," called one of the men to another who was smoking a pipe, " if you throw matches around near those

barrels of paper you'll have the old tin-
der-box burning down before you know
it." And Mrs. Manstey, leaning forward,
perceived that there were several barrels
of paper and rubbish under the wooden
balcony.

At length the work ceased and twilight
fell. The sunset was perfect and a rose-
ate light, transfiguring the distant spire,
lingered late in the west. When it grew
dark Mrs. Manstey drew down the shades
and proceeded, in her usual methodical
manner, to light her lamp. She always
filled and lit it with her own hands, keeping a kettle of kerosene on a zinc-covered
shelf in a closet. As the lamp-light filled
the room it assumed its peaceful aspect. The books and pictures and plants
seemed, like their mistress, to settle themselves down for another quiet evening,
and Mrs. Manstey, as was her wont, drew
up her armchair to the table and began to
knit.

That night she could not sleep. The
weather had changed and a wild wind
was abroad, blotting the stars with close-
driven clouds. Mrs. Manstey rose once or
twice and looked out of the window ; but
of the view nothing was discernible save a
tardy light or two in the opposite windows. These lights at last went out, and
Mrs. Manstey, who had watched for their
extinction, began to dress herself. She
was in evident haste, for she merely flung
a thin dressing-gown over her night-dress
and wrapped her head in a scarf; then
she opened her closet and cautiously took
out the kettle of kerosene. Having slipped
a bundle of wooden matches into her
pock t she proceeded, with increasing
precautions, to unlock her door, and a
few moments later she was feeling her
way down the dark staircase, led by a
glimmer of gas from the lower hall. At
length she reached the bottom of the
stairs and began the more difficult descent

into the utter darkness of the basement. Here, however, she could move more freely, as there was less danger of being overheard; and without much delay she contrived to unlock the iron door leading into the yard. A gust of cold wind smote her as she stepped out and groped shiveringly under the clothes-lines.

That morning at three o'clock an alarm of fire brought the engines to Mrs. Black's door, and also brought Mrs. Sampson's startled boarders to their windows. The wooden balcony at the back of Mrs. Black's house was ablaze, and among those who watched the progress of the flames was Mrs. Manstey, leaning in her thin dressing-gown from the open window.

The fire, however, was soon put out, and the frightened occupants of the house, who had fled in scant attire, reassembled at dawn to find that little mischief had been done beyond the cracking of window panes and smoking of ceilings. In fact, the chief sufferer by the fire was Mrs. Manstey, who was found in the morning gasping with pneumonia, a not unnatural result, as everyone remarked, of her having hung out of an open window at her age in a dressing-gown. It was easy to see that she was very ill, but no one had guessed how grave the doctor's verdict would be, and the faces gathered that evening about Mrs. Sampson's table were awe-struck and disturbed. Not that any of the borders knew Mrs. Manstey well; she " kept to herself," as they said, and seemed to fancy herself too good for them ; but then it is always disagreeable to have anyone dying in the house, and, as one lady observed to another: " It might just as well have been you or me, my dear."

But it was only Mrs. Manstey ; and she was dying, as she had lived, lonely if not alone. The doctor had sent a trained

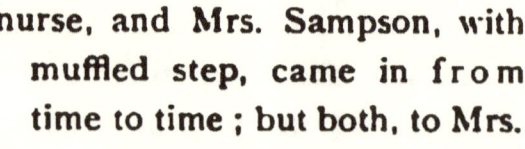

nurse, and Mrs. Sampson, with muffled step, came in from time to time ; but both, to Mrs. Manstey, seemed remote and unsubstantial as the figures in a dream. All day she said nothing ; but when she was asked for her daughter's address she shook her head. At times the nurse noticed that she seemed to be listening attentively for some sound which did not come ; then again she dozed.

The next morning at daylight she was very low. The nurse called Mrs. Sampson, and as the two bent over the old woman they saw her lips move.

"Lift me up—out of bed," she whispered.

They raised her in their arms, and with her stiff hand she pointed to the window.

" Oh, the window—she wants to sit in the window. She used to sit there all day," Mrs. Sampson explained. " It can do her no harm, I suppose ? "

" Nothing matters now," said the nurse.

They carried Mrs. Manstey to the window and placed her in her chair. The dawn was abroad, a jubilant spring dawn ; the spire had already caught a golden ray, though the magnolia and horse-chestnut still slumbered in shadow. In Mrs. Black's yard all was quiet. The charred timbers of the balcony lay where they had fallen. It was evident that since the fire the builders had not returned to their work. The magnolia had unfolded a few more sculptural flowers ; the view was undisturbed.

It was hard for Mrs. Manstey to breathe. Each moment it grew more difficult. She tried to make them open the

window, but they would not understand.
If she could have tasted the air, sweet
with the penetrating ailanthus savor, it
would have eased her ; but the view at
least was there—the spire was golden
now, the heavens had warmed from pearl
to blue, day was alight from east to west,
even the magnolia had caught the sun.

Mrs. Manstey's head fell back, and
smiling she died.

That day the building of the extension
was resumed.

STORIES FROM SCRIBNER

STORIES OF NEW YORK

NEW YORK
CHARLES SCRIBNER'S SONS
1893

In this series of little books, issued under the general title " Stories from Scribner," the purpose has been to gather together some of the best and most entertaining short stories written for Scribner's Magazine during the past few years, and to preserve them in dainty volumes grouped under attractive subjects and decorated by a few illustrations to brighten the pages.

The set as arranged consists of six volumes, the

first two appearing together and the other four at intervals of about a month, as follows :

Stories of New York.
Stories of the Railway.
Stories of the South.
Stories of the Sea.
Stories of Italy.
Stories of the Army.

The books are furnished in three bindings, the paper being the same in all. Each edition is prepared with great care, and every effort has been made to secure an example of book-making as dainty and perfect as possible.

The paper edition is enclosed in a transparent wrapper, fastened by a gold seal which should remain unbroken until the book reaches the hands of the reader. Price, 50 cents a volume.

The cloth edition has gilt top and rough edges. Price, 75 cents a volume.

The half calf edition is bound in the best leather and in two colors — blue and claret — gilt top. Price, $1.50 a volume.

Orders for the entire set may be sent to the publishers or to any bookseller.

CHARLES SCRIBNER'S SONS, New York.